Asterix Omnibus

ASTERIX THE GLADIATOR, ASTERIX AND THE BANQUET, ASTERIX AND CLEOPATRA

Written by RENÉ GOSCINNY

Illustrated by ALBERT UDERZO

Exclusive licensee: Orion Publishing Group
Translators: Anthea Bell and Derek Hockridge
Typography: Bryony Newhouse

Asterix the Gladiator
Original title: *Astérix Gladiateur*
Original edition © 1964 GOSCINNY/UDERZO
Revised edition and English translation © 2004 HACHETTE

Asterix and the Banquet
Original title: *Le Tour de Gaule d'Asterix*
Original edition © 1965 GOSCINNY/UDERZO
Revised edition and English translation © 2004 HACHETTE

Asterix and Cleopatra
Original title: Astérix et Cléopâtre
Original Edition © 1965 GOSCINNY/UDERZO
Revised edition and English translation © 2004 HACHETTE

This edition first published in Great Britain in 2008 by
Orion Books Ltd,
Orion House, 5 Upper St Martin's Lane
London WC2H 9EA
An Hachette Livre UK Company

Printed in France

http://gb.asterix.com
www.orionbooks.co.uk

A CIP catalogue record for this book is available from the British Library

ISBN 978 1 4091 0132 1 (Hardback)
ISBN 978 1 4091 0133 8 (Export Trade Paperback)

BELGICA

GAULISH VILLAGE

COMPENDIUM

LAUDANUM

AQUARIUM

TOTORUM

LUTETIA

ARMORICA

GAUL
(ROMAN CONQUEST)
50 BC

CELTICA

SPQR

AQUITANIA

PROVINCIA

THE YEAR IS 50 BC. GAUL IS ENTIRELY OCCUPIED BY THE
ROMANS. WELL, NOT ENTIRELY ... ONE SMALL VILLAGE OF
INDOMITABLE GAULS STILL HOLDS OUT AGAINST THE INVADERS.
AND LIFE IS NOT EASY FOR THE ROMAN LEGIONARIES WHO
GARRISON THE FORTIFIED CAMPS OF TOTORUM, AQUARIUM,
LAUDANUM AND COMPENDIUM ...

ASTERIX, THE HERO OF THESE ADVENTURES. A SHREWD, CUNNING LITTLE WARRIOR, ALL PERILOUS MISSIONS ARE IMMEDIATELY ENTRUSTED TO HIM. ASTERIX GETS HIS SUPERHUMAN STRENGTH FROM THE MAGIC POTION BREWED BY THE DRUID GETAFIX . . .

OBELIX, ASTERIX'S INSEPARABLE FRIEND. A MENHIR DELIVERY MAN BY TRADE, ADDICTED TO WILD BOAR. OBELIX IS ALWAYS READY TO DROP EVERYTHING AND GO OFF ON A NEW ADVENTURE WITH ASTERIX – SO LONG AS THERE'S WILD BOAR TO EAT, AND PLENTY OF FIGHTING. HIS CONSTANT COMPANION IS DOGMATIX, THE ONLY KNOWN CANINE ECOLOGIST, WHO HOWLS WITH DESPAIR WHEN A TREE IS CUT DOWN.

GETAFIX, THE VENERABLE VILLAGE DRUID, GATHERS MISTLETOE AND BREWS MAGIC POTIONS. HIS SPECIALITY IS THE POTION WHICH GIVES THE DRINKER SUPERHUMAN STRENGTH. BUT GETAFIX ALSO HAS OTHER RECIPES UP HIS SLEEVE . . .

CACOFONIX, THE BARD. OPINION IS DIVIDED AS TO HIS MUSICAL GIFTS. CACOFONIX THINKS HE'S A GENIUS. EVERY-ONE ELSE THINKS HE'S UNSPEAKABLE. BUT SO LONG AS HE DOESN'T SPEAK, LET ALONE SING, EVERYBODY LIKES HIM . . .

FINALLY, VITALSTATISTIX, THE CHIEF OF THE TRIBE. MAJESTIC, BRAVE AND HOT-TEMPERED, THE OLD WARRIOR IS RESPECTED BY HIS MEN AND FEARED BY HIS ENEMIES. VITALSTATISTIX HIMSELF HAS ONLY ONE FEAR, HE IS AFRAID THE SKY MAY FALL ON HIS HEAD TOMORROW. BUT AS HE ALWAYS SAYS, TOMORROW NEVER COMES.

R. GOSCINNY

A. UDERZO

Asterix the gladiator

Written by René GOSCINNY

Illustrated by Albert UDERZO

UDERZO

GOSCINNY AND UDERZO
PRESENT
An Asterix Adventure

ASTERIX
THE
GLADIATOR

Written by RENÉ GOSCINNY *and Illustrated by* ALBERT UDERZO

Translated by Anthea Bell *and* Derek Hockridge

THE ROMAN CAMP OF COMPENDIUM IS IN A FERMENT. THE PREFECT OF GAUL, ODIUS ASPARAGUS, IS PAYING A CALL ON CENTURION GRACCHUS ARMISURPLUS. THE PREFECT ARRIVES FROM THE NEARBY COAST WHERE HIS GALLEY HAS PUT IN...

PRESENT... PILUM!...

AVE, PREFECT! THIS IS A GREAT HONOUR FOR ME!

AVE, CENTURION! YOU'RE TELLING ME!

AND NOW FOR THE PURPOSE OF MY VISIT, CENTURION! I'M GOING TO ROME ON LEAVE, AND CUSTOM DECREES THAT I TAKE CAESAR A HANDSOME PRESENT... SOMETHING UNUSUAL AND VERY VALUABLE...

...I DID THINK OF TAKING HIM A PRESENT FROM LUTETIA, MAYBE A MARBLE MEMO TABLET FOR HIM TO CARVE DOWN HIS APPOINTMENTS, BUT THAT'S TOO ORDINARY...

THEN I HAD A BRILLIANT IDEA! WHY NOT TAKE CAESAR ONE OF THE INVINCIBLE GAULS FROM HEREABOUTS?

WHAT?!

BUT, PREFECT, ABOUT THESE INVINCIBLE GAULS... THERE'S JUST ONE SNAG!

WELL, WHAT IS IT?

THEY HAPPEN TO BE INVINCIBLE!

THAT'S WHAT MAKES THEM SO VALUABLE! GET ME ONE OF THESE GAULS, AND YOU WON'T REGRET IT!

THERE'S CERTAINLY ONE WHO'S A BIT MORE HARMLESS THAN THE OTHERS... CACOFONIX THE BARD. HE OFTEN GOES FOR WALKS IN THE FOREST BY HIMSELF LOOKING FOR INSPIRATION!

EXCELLENT! I MUST HAVE THIS BARD – AND FAST!

AND IN THE GAULISH VILLAGE...

GOODBYE, ASTERIX, I'M GOING FOR A WALK IN THE FOREST!

GOODBYE, CACOFONIX!

13

PHEW! THAT'S THAT!

HMMMMM!

WHAT DID YOU SAY?

TAKE THAT PARSLEY OUT OF YOUR EARS!

?!

AVE! MISSION ACCOMPLISHED! WE CAPTURED THE GAULISH BARD AT THE RISK OF OUR LIVES. ESPECIALLY MINE!

EXCELLENT! EXCELLENT!

THERE, IT WASN'T ALL THAT DIFFICULT...

THE TROUBLE IS WE CAN NOW EXPECT REPRISALS FROM THE OTHERS...

OH... ER... WELL, YES... WELL, I REALLY MUST BE GOING! FETCH MY LITTER! THE PRISONER AND I WILL LEAVE AT ONCE TO GO ON BOARD THE GALLEY FOR ROME...

MEANWHILE...

THAT'S GOOD NEWS, BUT I DON'T SUPPOSE HE'LL BE LONG.

OBELIX, OUR BARD CACOFONIX HASN'T COME BACK YET.

ASTERIX! ASTERIX! I SAW SOME ROMANS CAPTURING CACOFONIX!

ARE YOU SURE, PICANMIX?

I WAS OUT HUNTING WILD PIGLETS IN THE FOREST, AND I SAW IT ALL!

WHAT A FUNNY IDEA OF THE ROMANS'! WHYEVER SHOULD THEY WANT TO LUMBER THEMSELVES WITH CACOFONIX?

ANYWAY, WE MUST AVENGE THIS INSULT! I'M OFF TO TELL OUR CHIEF VITALSTATISTIX THE NEWS!

OBELIX QUARRY
CAUTION
MENHIRS TURNING

HIGHER!

O VITALSTATISTIX, OUR BARD CACOFONIX HAS DISAPPEARED!

YOU'RE JUST SAYING THAT TO PLEASE ME...

THE ROMANS HAVE CAPTURED HIM!

WHAT?

BY TOUTATIS! EVEN IF IT IS A FUNNY IDEA OF THE ROMANS', THAT'S NOT PLAYING FAIR! WE CAN'T HAVE THIS SORT OF THING!

A GAUL MUST KNOW HOW TO MAKE HIS ENEMY RESPECT HIM! WE SHALL ORGANISE A PUNITIVE EXPEDITION! LET THE DRUID PREPARE THE MAGIC POTION!

SOON AFTERWARDS THE GAULISH WARRIORS ARE DRINKING THE MAGIC POTION WHICH GIVES THEM INVINCIBLE STRENGTH...

NO, OBELIX! NOT YOU! I'VE ALREADY TOLD YOU YOU DON'T NEED ANY POTION! YOU'RE STRONG ENOUGH AS YOU ARE!

WHAT, ME STRONG? NOT A BIT OF IT! I'M AS WEAK AS ANYTHING!

GO ON! I'LL GIVE YOU THIS NICE MENHIR!

NO, NO, AND FOR THE THIRD TIME NO!

SILENCE! OUR CHIEF VITALSTATISTIX IS GOING TO MAKE A SPEECH!

FRIENDS, GAULS, COUNTRYMEN! WE MUST GIVE THESE ROMANS A GOOD LESSON, BY TOUTATIS!

AND REMEMBER, WE HAVE NOTHING TO FEAR BUT THE SKY FALLING ON OUR HEADS!

IN THE ROMAN CAMP OF COMPENDIUM THE TROOPS HAVE BEEN ALERTED...

AND REMEMBER, ROMANS, WE HAVE NOTHING TO FEAR BUT THE GAULS!

THIS IS THE FIRST TIME CACOFONIX HAS EVER GIVEN US ANY ENTERTAINMENT!

I SAY, ASTERIX! HOW ABOUT A BET? THE ONE WHO KNOCKS OUT MOST LEGIONARIES WINS, AND WE HAVE TO COLLECT THEIR HELMETS AS PROOF!

AT THIS VERY MOMENT, AT COMPENDIUM...

PUT YOUR HELMETS ON!!!

THE GALL...GAULS! SOUND THE ALARM!

HELP! THEY'RE COMING!

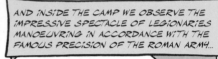

AND INSIDE THE CAMP WE OBSERVE THE IMPRESSIVE SPECTACLE OF LEGIONARIES MANOEUVRING IN ACCORDANCE WITH THE FAMOUS PRECISION OF THE ROMAN ARMY...

COHORTS INTO THREE LINES... FORM!

SOUND THE HORNS, TRUMPETS AND BUCINAS!

PILUM AT THE READY!

MANOEUVRE, BY JUPITER!!!

WHOOOOOOSH!

WE CAN'T! THE GAULS ARE IN THE WAY!

THE BATTLE IS SHORT...

BANG! CLINK CLANK CLONK! BIFF!

BUT SHARP...

SWOOOSH!

I CAN'T FIND CACOFONIX ANYWHERE... AH, THERE'S THE ROMAN COMMANDER!

BANG! BING!

I SHALL FIGHT TO THE DEATH!

WANT ME TO THUMP YOU?

OH ALL RIGHT! ALL IS LOST! I SURRENDER! ALEA JACTA EST!

AND LET IT BE A LESSON TO YOU! NOW, GIVE US BACK OUR BARD, AND DON'T DO IT AGAIN!

THE FACT IS... YOUR BARD ISN'T HERE ANY MORE. AT THIS MOMENT HE'S ON BOARD A GALLEY, SAILING FOR ROME TO BE GIVEN TO CAESAR AS A PRESENT...

!!!

WE'RE WASTING OUR TIME...

A PRESENT? THAT'S A REALLY FUNNY IDEA!

LOOK AT THIS, ASTERIX! I'M SURE I'VE WON OUR BET! AND ONE LEGIONARY WAS FIGHTING BARE-HEADED TOO. IT'S AGAINST ALL THE RULES OF WARFARE TO GO INTO BATTLE IMPROPERLY DRESSED! I'VE A GOOD MIND TO REPORT HIM!

THE GAULS WITHDRAW, LEAVING BEHIND THEM THE AFTERMATH OF BATTLE...

THEY REALLY LET US HAVE IT, EH, SIR?

IN THE FIRST PLACE, GET THIS CAMP BACK INTO ORDER!!! WHAT'S ALL THIS UNTIDINESS IN AID OF? AND DON'T ANYONE EVER MENTION THIS BATTLE TO ME AGAIN!!!

LATER, IN THE GAULISH VILLAGE...

POOR CACOFONIX, PRISONER ON BOARD A ROMAN GALLEY!

HE WAS SO NICE! SCRUNCH! SO WELL BROUGHT UP! NEVER SANG WITH HIS MOUTH FULL! SCRUNCH! PITY HE DIDN'T EAT MUCH... SCRUNCH!

MEANWHILE...

I CAN'T WAIT TO GIVE YOU TO CAESAR!

YOUR CAESAR DOESN'T DESERVE ME, ROMAN!

MAKE THEM ROW FASTER!

BONG! BONG!

BONG! BONG!

CRACK! CRACK!

STOP HAVING THOSE UNHAPPY SOULS WHIPPED, ROMAN! LOOSEN SOME OF MY BONDS! I WILL SING A SONG TO LIVEN THEM UP!

?!

FAREWELL AND ADIEU TO YOU FAIR CELTIC LADIES...

FAREWELL AND ADIEU TO YOU LADIES OF GAUL...

CLICK! CLACK! CLONK! CLUNK! BOING

STOP! MERCY!

WE'D RATHER HAVE THE WHIP!

OUR WORK ISN'T ALL FUN AND GAMES, BUT THIS IS INHUMAN! IF THE GAUL WILL SHUT UP WE PROMISE TO ROW OUR HARDEST!

YOU IGNORANT LOT! YOU BRUTES! YOU'LL ALL END UP IN THE... WELL, YOU ALREADY HAVE!

BONG

I'M BEGINNING TO WONDER IF CAESAR REALLY DOES DESERVE THIS...

20

OBELIX! WE MUST GO TO ROME AND RESCUE CACOFONIX!

THAT'S ALL RIGHT BY ME... SCRUNCH! SCRUNCH! ...BUT HOW DO WE GET THERE? IT'S A LONG WAY! SCRUNCH!

...AND SO WE'LL GO DOWN TO THE BEACH AND TAKE THE FIRST BOAT FOR ROME!

IT'S RISKY, ASTERIX, BUT YOU'RE RIGHT; WE CAN'T LEAVE OUR BARD IN THE LURCH. HE SINGS ATROCIOUSLY, BUT HE'S A GOOD SORT...

AN EXCELLENT SORT!

YOU COME WITH ME, ASTERIX, AND I'LL MAKE YOU A GOURD OF MAGIC POTION...

I'LL JUST GO AND FIND SOMEONE TO DELIVER MY MENHIRS WHILE I'M AWAY...

I DON'T KNOW THAT I'M CUT OUT FOR THIS SORT OF WORK...

I'M RELYING ON YOU. YOU NEEDN'T DELIVER MORE THAN ONE AT A TIME TO START WITH.

COME ON, OBELIX, IT'S TIME TO LEAVE!

COMING, ASTERIX!

TAKE CARE!

DON'T WORRY! IF THE ROMANS AREN'T NICE TO US WE'LL LEAVE THEIR CITY FULL OF RUINS!

ASTERIX, WHAT'S THE LATIN FOR WILD BOAR?

SINGULARIS PORCUS, BUT I DON'T KNOW IF THEY HAVE THEM IN ROME.

NOW WE HAVE TO WAIT FOR A SHIP...

LET'S HAVE A BET WHILE WE WAIT. WE SEE HOW MANY DOZEN OYSTERS WE CAN EAT, AND THE ONE WHO EATS MOST WINS A SINGULARIS PORCUS!

LOOK! A SHIP! WE'RE IN LUCK!

WHY DON'T WE WAIT FOR THE NEXT ONE? THEN WE COULD HAVE OUR BET!

NOW TO STOP THIS SHIP SAILING ALONG THE COAST!

ASTERIX AND OBELIX MAKE THE ANCIENT GAULISH SIGN INDICATING A WISH TO BE TAKEN ON BOARD. NOTE THE FOUR CLENCHED FINGERS AND THE THUMB JERKED IN THE DESIRED DIRECTION. IF YOU WISH TO GO TO ROME, THE DIRECTION OF THE THUMB IS IMMATERIAL, SINCE ALL ROADS LEAD THERE.

N.B. THIS GESTURE IS STILL EMPLOYED TODAY, THOUGH NOT OFTEN TO STOP SHIPS.

IT'S A PHOENICIAN GALLEY. THE PHOENICIANS ARE FAMOUS SAILORS AND MERCHANTS!

WHAT'S THE PHOENICIAN FOR SINGULARIS PORCUS?

WE'RE FROM TYRE IN PHOENICIA. MY NAME IS EKONOMIKRISIS. WOULD YOU LIKE TO BUY ANY GLASS, JEWELS, TEXTILES, PURPLE, FURNITURE?

NO, WE WANT TO GO TO ROME.

HM... ER... ALL RIGHT, COME ON BOARD!

ARE THOSE SLAVES?

OH NO, THEY'RE PARTNERS... WHEN WE FLOATED THE COMPANY, I DREW UP THE CONTRACT AND THEY FAILED TO READ IT CAREFULLY BEFORE SIGNING. I'M CHAIRMAN AND MANAGING DIRECTOR.

IT'S KIND OF YOU TO TAKE US TO ROME. I HOPE IT DOESN'T MEAN GOING OUT OF YOUR WAY?

AS IT HAPPENS, WE WERE PLANNING TO GO TO ROME. ONE OF MY PREDECESSORS ABANDONED HIS SHIP THERE...

IT SANK?

NO, HE SOLD IT. HE WAS A BETTER SALESMAN THAN SAILSMAN.

A SAIL ON THE HORIZON, MR. CHAIRMAN!

IT MUST BE PIRATES! THEY MAY TAKE US PRISONER, KILL US, OR EVEN WORSE, STEAL OUR MERCHANDISE!

SURE ENOUGH, ON BOARD THE PIRATE GALLEY...

SHIVER ME TIMBERS, WE'VE GOT 'EM ME HEARTIES! PULL AWAY! THAT HEAVY PHOENICIAN SHIP WITH ALL ITS CARGO WILL NEVER ESCAPE US!

LET'S PUSH THE BOAT OUT!

TEEHEEHEE!

MY DEAR FELLOW DIRECTORS, I THINK WE SHALL BE OBLIGED TO FIGHT...

NO, NO, MR. CHAIRMAN! OUR CONTRACT SAYS WE HAVE TO ROW, BUT THERE'S NOTHING IN THE SMALL PRINT ABOUT FIGHTING!

NOW, I SUGGEST WE CHANGE THE CONTRACT. I HAVE AN IMPORTANT MODIFICATION TO MAKE.

ME TOO!

ME TOO!

ME TOO!

ME TOO!

ME TOO!

ME TOO!

ME TOO!

WE CAN'T COUNT ON THESE CHATTERBOXES TO FIGHT. WE'LL HAVE TO DEAL WITH THIS ON OUR OWN.

GOODY! THERE'LL BE MORE ROOM! LOOK, HERE COME THE PIRATES. POOR THINGS!

THEY'RE WEARING HELMETS! WE CAN HAVE ANOTHER BET LIKE WE DID WITH THE LEGIONARIES!

+24

GIDDY GOAT'S HORNS, WE'LL MAKE JUST ONE MOUTHFUL OF THEM!

VANITAS VANITATUM ET OMNIA VANITAS!

WE MIGHT ON THE ONE HAND HOLD AN EXTRAORDINARY GENERAL MEETING TO DISCUSS THE TERMS OF THE CONTRACT, WHILE ALTERNATIVELY, ON THE OTHER HAND...

WELL, I THINK THIS WOULD BE A VERY GOOD MOMENT TO...

11

23

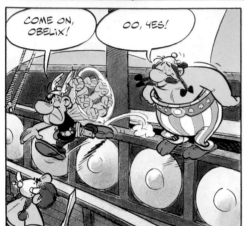

YOU HAVE SAVED WHAT IS DEAREST TO OUR HEARTS — OUR CARGO! NOW WE'RE BOSOM FRIENDS!

I ORIGINALLY INTENDED TO SELL YOU AS SLAVES WHEN WE CALLED AT THE NEXT PORT. BUT NOW I'LL TAKE YOU TO ROME AS AGREED.

YOU CERTAINLY DO HAVE BUSINESS ACUMEN!

WHAT CAN YOU EXPECT? AS I WAS SAYING TO MY PARTNERS, WE'RE ALL IN THE SAME BOAT, AND WE MUSTN'T REST ON OUR OARS IF OUR OVERHEADS ARE NOT TO MAKE US GO UNDER!

MEANWHILE, IN ROME...

AVE, CAESAR!

AVE, ODIUS ASPARAGUS, PREFECT OF GAUL.

HERE'S MY PRESENT, O CAESAR! A GAULISH BARD FROM THE TRIBE OF INDOMITABLE GAULS IN THE COMPENDIUM AREA.

I'VE BEEN BROUGHT HERE AS A SOUVENIR... JUST AS IF I WAS A VULGAR PAINTED SHELL!

A BARD? HOW INTERESTING!

YOU CAN WAIT TILL THE COWS COME HOME BEFORE I'LL SING FOR YOU... AND YOU DON'T KNOW WHAT YOU'RE MISSING!

THANKS FOR THIS ORIGINAL LITTLE PRESENT, PREFECT. YOU MAY GO!

SEND FOR CAIUS FATUOUS, THE LANISTA *

* TRAINER OF THE GLADIATORS

CAIUS FATUOUS, CAN YOU MAKE A GLADIATOR OF THIS BARD?

DEAR ME, NO, O CAESAR! HE'S TOO WEAK... NOT ENOUGH MEAT ON HIM.

IF I WASN'T RESTRAINING MYSELF...

VERY WELL THEN, THROW HIM TO THE LIONS AT THE NEXT GAMES, TAKE HIM AWAY!

27

WELL, SO WE'VE GOT A DATE AT INSTANTMIX'S PLACE THIS EVENING. WHAT DO WE DO TILL THEN?

WE COULD GO BACK AND HAVE SOME MORE BOAR?

BOAR ON THE SPIT

THE BATHS! I'VE OFTEN HEARD ABOUT THE ROMAN BATHS! LET'S GO AND HAVE A BATH!

THERMAE

GO AND GET UNDRESSED IN THE APODYTERIA.

THAT MUST MEAN THE CHANGING ROOM...

THIS WAY, NOBLE LORDS!

IS IT US HE MEANS?

APODYTERIA

WE HAVEN'T GOT MUCH ON. I HOPE WE DON'T CATCH COLD!

SVDATORIA

IT'S HOT IN HERE!

I WONDER IF WE COULD OPEN A WINDOW.

LOOK, CAIUS FATUOUS! YOU'RE ALWAYS ON THE LOOKOUT FOR GLADIATORS – WHAT DO YOU THINK OF THOSE TWO MEN?

INTERESTING. ESPECIALLY THE FAT ONE.

LET'S TRY IN HERE... IT MAY BE COOLER.

THIS WAS A FUNNY IDEA OF YOURS, ASTERIX, BY TOUTATIS!

HE SAID 'BY TOUTATIS' ... THEY'RE GAULS...

CALDARIVM

WE MAY BE HARD-BOILED, BUT THIS IS OVERDOING IT!

YOU SEEM TO BE STRANGERS HERE. I'LL GUIDE YOU ROUND THE BATHS. I COME HERE REGULARLY FOR MY HEALTH, THOUGH IT IS A BIT OF A SWEAT...

YOU SHOULD GO TO THE FRIGIDARIUM AND DIVE INTO THE POOL OF ICY WATER.

ICY WATER? I'M ON MY WAY!

WATCH ME DIVE, ASTERIX! WATCH ME DIVE!

16

29

THIS INN OPPOSITE THE *CIRCUS* WILL SUIT US NICELY. LET'S SEE IF THEY HAVE ANY ROOM.

RIGHT.

I WONDER IF THEY'LL LET US IN AT THIS TIME OF NIGHT...

I'LL JUST KNOCK...

SOON AFTERWARDS...

THAT WILL BE 20 SESTERTII FOR THE NIGHT AND 40 SESTERTII FOR THE DOOR.

MEANWHILE, IN THE HOUSE OF CAIUS FATUOUS THE GLADIATOR TRAINER...

WELL, DID YOU GET THEM?

ER... NO, BOSS... THEY DIDN'T WANT TO COME.

I MUST HAVE THOSE TWO MEN! JUMP TO IT, EVERYONE!

AND NEXT MORNING...

SLEEP WELL, ASTERIX?

YES, THANK YOU, OBELIX. LET'S GO AND HAVE BREAKFAST NOW.

WE MUST TRY TO GET INTO CONVERSATION WITH ONE OF THE CIRCUS GUARDS AND FIND OUT EXACTLY WHERE CACOFONIX IS IMPRISONED!

WAITER! HAVE YOU BY ANY CHANCE GOT SOME PARSLEY?

PARSLEY? WHAT FOR?

FOR PUTTING IN MY EARS! I'VE GOT A PRISONER WHO KEEPS ON SINGING, SOMETHING HORRIBLE!

THAT'S CACOFONIX!

THE DESCRIPTION FITS, ANYWAY!

20

LET'S TRY A FEW CRAFTY QUESTIONS ON THIS GUARD. WE MUSTN'T AROUSE HIS SUSPICIONS...

NO...

HEY, YOU! WHERE'S CACOFONIX IMPRISONED?

?!

CELL XVIII, FIRST BASEMENT DOWN, BUT IT'S A SECRET!

THERE!

SOON AFTERWARDS...

AND NOW FOR THE CIRCUS. I'LL DRINK A LITTLE MAGIC POTION.

HERE'S MY PLAN — WE KNOCK DOWN EVERYONE AND EVERYTHING UNTIL WE FIND CACOFONIX AND THEN WE MAKE OFF WITH HIM!

THAT'S A CLEVER PLAN!

HALT!
NO...

ENTRY!

CELL XV... CELL XVI... CELL XVII... WE'RE GETTING WARM!

OUR BET ABOUT THE HELMETS IS STILL ON, ISN'T IT?

CELL XVIII IS EMPTY!

HEY! WHAT ARE YOU TWO DOING HERE?

21

WHERE'S THE BARD, GUARD?

THEY CHANGED HIS CELL. HE'S SOMEWHERE IN THE THIRD BASEMENT DOWN. NO ONE COULD BEAR TO HEAR HIM ANY MORE. PLEASE WOULD YOU KINDLY STOP HITTING ME!

BIFF! BIFF! BIFF! BIFF!

SOUND THE ALARM!

COME ON THEN!

NO! WE MUST GET OUT OF HERE!

...EXIT!

BIFF!

LET'S GO AND ASK OUR FRIEND INSTANTMIX'S ADVICE...

WELL, WHAT **WERE** THOSE TWO AFTER ANYWAY?

SOON AFTERWARDS...

I WARNED YOU! ONLY CONDEMNED MEN, LIONS AND GLADIATORS GET INTO THAT CIRCUS!

SNIFF! SNIFF!

MEANWHILE, IN THE HOUSE OF CAIUS FATUOUS...

TWO GAULS TRYING TO RESCUE THE BARD? THOSE MUST CERTAINLY BE MY MEN, AND THEY MUST CERTAINLY BE INDOMITABLE GAULS!

I WANT THE WHOLE STAFF TO COMB THE CITY IN GROUPS OF THREE! I MUST HAVE THOSE TWO GAULS! BRING THEM TO ME!

AND IF THAT DOESN'T WORK, PUT UP NOTICES EVERYWHERE! I'M OFFERING 10,000 SESTERTII TO ANYONE WHO CAPTURES THESE TWO INDOMITABLE GAULS!

YES, BOSS!

SOON AFTERWARDS...

THERE THEY ARE!

GAULISH RESTAURANT

WINES OF AQUITANIA AND NARBONNE

LUGDUNUM SAUSAGE

BOAR ON THE SPIT

22

LET'S GET THEM!

SPLAT!

IT'S A NUISANCE, WHAT INSTANTMIX TOLD US...

CLONK!

YES, HEARING THINGS LIKE THAT MAKES ME COME OVER ALL FAINT

HE SAID ONLY CONDEMNED MEN, LIONS AND GLADIATORS GET INTO THE CIRCUS...

SUPPOSE WE DRESSED UP AS LIONS?

GAULISH RESTAURANT

HERE THEY COME!

YOU'RE TOO FAT FOR A LION!

IF ONLY I'D KNOWN...

ALL THE SAME, WE MUST SAVE OUR BARD!

OF COURSE!

LET'S BEAT IT! HERE COME THE COPS!

NOW, NOW, NOW, WHAT'S ALL THIS 'ERE? YOU COME ALONG QUIETLY TO THE STATION! AND NO FUNNY BUSINESS – WE'RE SEVEN TO TWO!

LET'S GET BACK TO OUR INN!

FORWARD, MEN... OUFF!

I SAY, ASTERIX, DON'T YOU THINK IT'S FUNNY, ALL THESE PEOPLE ATTACKING US?

PEOPLE? WHAT PEOPLE?

CIRCUS INN

23

TEN THOUSAND SESTERTII

TEN THOUSAND SESTERTII

FOR THE CAPTURE OF TWO DANGEROUS GAULS: ONE SMALL FAIR MAN, BIG MOUSTACHE, WINGED HELMET. ONE FAT GINGER-HAIRED MAN, BIG MOUSTACHE, PIGTAILS.

CAIUS FATUOUS LANISTA

IN THE CIRCUS INN...

OBELIX, I'VE JUST HAD AN IDEA! WE'LL BECOME GLADIATORS!

OH?

AND HOW DO WE GET TO BE GLADIATORS?

WE'LL ASK A ROMAN... THE ONLY ONE WE KNOW IS THAT ONE WHO HAS A LOT OF BATHS. LET'S GO TO THE BATHS!

AND OUTSIDE THE BATHS...

10,000 SESTERTII... THAT'S A LOT OF MONEY!

I COULD JUST DO WITH THAT!

THERMAE

LOOK!

I SAW THEM FIRST!

NO, ME!

?!???

IT'S A LIE! THE 10,000 SESTERTII ARE MINE!

HERE, LET US BY! WE'RE IN A HURRY.

THESE ROMANS ARE CRAZY!

OH, SO IT'S YOU TWO BACK AGAIN. I THOUGHT I TOLD YOU BEFORE...

OI! TAKE YOUR SANDALS OFF IF YOU WANT TO COME IN THE BATH!

SPLOSH!

I MUST FIRST WIN THEIR CONFIDENCE SO THAT THEY'LL SIGN THE CONTRACT WHICH WILL GET THEM INTO MY HOT LITTLE HANDS...

COME ALONG IN... WE'LL HAVE A LIGHT MEAL.

NICE PLACE YOU'VE GOT HERE!

COULDN'T WE HAVE A HEAVY MEAL INSTEAD?

JUST TASTE THESE PASTIES! THEY'RE A NEW RECIPE – THEY COST A FORTUNE! NIGHTINGALES' TONGUES IMPORTED FROM THE NORTH OF GAUL, STURGEONS' EGGS FROM THE FARTHEST BARBARIAN LANDS, COCKROACHES' GUMS FROM MONGOLIA...

WELL, WHAT DO YOU THINK OF THEM?

GULP!

SALTY.

!

RIGHT! THE FUN'S OVER, BY JUPITER! MAKE YOUR MARKS ON THESE CONTRACTS!

EXCELLENT! UP YOU GET! INSALUBRIUS!

INSALUBRIUS, HERE ARE THE TWO NEW GLADIATORS! TRAIN THEM FOR THE CIRCUS – AND JUMP TO IT!

THEY'LL JUMP TO IT ALL RIGHT, LANISTA, THEY'LL JUMP TO IT!

I SAY, ASTERIX, DO YOU THINK THE LIGHT MEAL'S OVER?

SALTY! HUH! THESE BARBARIANS DON'T APPRECIATE GOOD FOOD! BRING ME THE GIBLET JAM!

SNAP!

26

41

WH... WHAT'S THIS? YOU'VE GOT OUT??

NOT A BAD PROGRAMME, BUT WE'LL WANT TO MAKE A FEW ALTERATIONS...

HE DOES SEEM SURPRISED TO SEE US! AND PLEASED!

with
ASTERIX & OBELIX
THE INDOMITABLE GAULS
(BOOKING OFFICE NOW OPEN)

YOU TURNED UP JUST AT THE RIGHT MOMENT! WE WERE LOOKING FOR A GUIDE TO SHOW US THE TOWN!

A GUI... A GUI... A GUIDE!

SLAP!

KEEP A STIFF UPPER LIP... THE MAIN THING IS NOT TO LOSE SIGHT OF THEM...

ALL RIGHT.

...AND THIS IS THE FORUM.

PITY WE CAN'T TAKE PICTURES OF ALL THIS BACK TO GAUL WITH US...

TOURIST GUIDE

SOUVENIRS

YOU SEEM VERY SURE YOU'LL GET OUT OF THE CIRCUS ALIVE!

WELL, OF COURSE!

DON'T YOU WORRY ABOUT US!

?!?

SUPPOSE I WENT CARVING MY NAME ON YOUR PYRAMIDS, EH?

NOW LET'S GO BACK TO YOUR PLACE FOR DINNER!

AND NO BORING LITTLE PASTIES THIS TIME – JUST BOARS!

DINNER IS MUCH ENJOYED BY EVERYONE – WELL, NEARLY EVERYONE...

I'LL SAY ONE THING FOR THE ROMANS, THEY KNOW HOW TO ENTERTAIN! ISN'T THAT RIGHT, OBELIX?

YUM! GULP! 'SRIGHT! SCRUNCH!

PATIENCE, PATIENCE! THEY'LL BE LAUGHING THE OTHER SIDE OF THEIR FACES IN THE ARENA!

COME ALONG, IT'S TIME TO GO BACK TO OUR QUARTERS! I HOPE WE HAVEN'T OVERSTAYED OUR WELCOME?

I SHOULD HAVE HAD A BOAR FOR THE ROAD...

31

TIME PASSES BY, AND THE GLADIATORS ARE PUTTING ON WEIGHT...

MY FIRST IS A HUNDRED, MY SECOND IS A SIGN OF THE ZODIAC, MY THIRD IS A HIBERNIAN, MY FOURTH IS THE EGYPTIAN GOD OF THE SUN AND JULIUS CAESAR LOVES MY WHOLE! WHO AM I?

WHILE CAIUS FATUOUS IS LOSING IT...

THERE THEY GO AGAIN! PLAYING IDIOTIC GAMES INSTEAD OF TRAINING! A FINE CIRCUS THIS IS GOING TO BE!

IT'S C, LEO, PAT, RA... CLEOPATRA!

THAT WAS A DIFFICULT ONE, THAT WAS!

THE GAMES ARE FIXED FOR TOMORROW. THIS WILL BE YOUR LAST NIGHT IN THE CIRCUS, YOU USELESS LOT!

WE DON'T REALLY WANT TO FIGHT ANY MORE, ASTERIX.

DON'T WORRY! I PROMISE YOU WON'T HAVE TO RISK YOUR LIVES IN THE ARENA!

AND A VERY RELAXED GROUP OF GLADIATORS ARRIVES AT THE CIRCUS...

HA, HA! HO, HO!

STOP PUSHING, WILL YOU!

PORPUS IS A BEAST! PASS IT ON!

WHAT'S THE MATTER WITH THEM?

NO IDEA. LOCK THEM UP DOWN BELOW!

PORTER, WE WANT TO SEE OUR FRIEND CACOFONIX THE BARD.

I'M NOT A PORTER AND YOU CAN'T!

VERY WELL THEN, WE SHALL TEAR OUT THESE BARS ONE BY ONE UNTIL YOU CO-OPERATE!

GO AHEAD AND TRY!

PLINNNK!

PLONNNK!

PLUNNNK!

STOP! LEAVE THE FIXTURES ALONE!

AH, ABOUT TIME TOO! WHAT SERVICE!

32

A HUGE CROWD IS FORMING OUTSIDE THE CIRCUS...

WASH YOUR TOGAS IN SUPER PERSIC! SUPER PERSIC WASHES EVEN PURPLER!

SCORE CARD! SCORE CARD!

CUSHIONS! CUSHIONS!

CHIPOLATAE! CANES CALIDI! CHIPOLATAE!

AND INSIDE THE IMPOSING ARENA THE TRUMPETS ANNOUNCE THE ARRIVAL OF CAESAR IN THE IMPERIAL BOX...

TANTAN TARA!!!!

PANEM ET CIRCENSES

LONG LIVE CAESAR!

CAESAR FOR EVER!

EVERYONE APPLAUDS THE DICTATOR...

CLAP! CLAP! CLAP! CLAP! CLAP! CLAP!

CLAP! CLAP! CLAP! CLAP! CLAP! CLAP! CLAP!

ET TU BRUTE!*

CLAP! CLAP! CLAP!

CLAP! CLAP! CLAP! CLAP! CLAP!

* YOU TOO, BRUTUS!

THAT BRUTUS... I CAN SEE I'M GOING TO HAVE TROUBLE WITH HIM.*

CLAP! CLAP! CLAP! CLAP! CLAP! CLAP! CLAP! CLAP!

* AN EXAMINATION OF ACT III, SCENE 1 OF JULIUS CAESAR BY WILLIAM SHAKESPEARE WILL INDICATE THE PROPHETIC NATURE OF THIS REMARK.

THIS WILL BE A GREAT SHOW, O CAESAR!

I HOPE SO, CAIUS FATUOUS. IF NOT, YOU'LL BE IN ON THE ACT.

LET THE GAMES BEGIN!

GULP!—

34

48

SO YOU WANT TO SEE SOME FIGHTING, ROMAN? THEN YOU SHALL! SEND IN SOME OF YOUR CRACK LEGIONARIES. MY FRIEND OBELIX AND I WILL DEAL WITH THEM. LEAVE THOSE OTHER POOR DEVILS ALONE!

OH, SO YOU WANT TO MAKE FUN OF ME, GAULS? VERY WELL! **SEND IN A COHORT OF MY BEST LEGIONARIES!!!**

THE REST OF YOU GO AND PLAY OUTSIDE...

YES, BUT WAS I OUT OR NOT?

I'LL JUST FINISH OFF THE MAGIC POTION...

SHALL WE DO THE HELMET ROUTINE AGAIN? SHALL WE, ASTERIX?

WELL, ARE THEY COMING OR DO WE HAVE TO GO AND FETCH THEM?

GOODY! HERE THEY COME, ALL WITH THEIR TIN HATS ON!

LEFT, RIGHT

UNARMED! I WANT TO PROLONG THE PLEASURE! I WANT TO SEE YOU FLATTEN THESE TWO GAULS WITH YOUR BARE HANDS!

I PROTEST! IT WON'T BE A FAIR FIGHT IF THEY'RE UNARMED!

BOING!

BONG! BANG! BING!

YOU COMING? I'VE STARTED ALREADY!

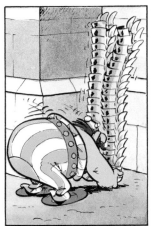

...AND FINALLY I ASK YOU TO FREE THE GLADIATORS. THEY'RE GIVING UP THEIR BLOODTHIRSTY JOB!

GRANTED, O GAUL!

MMPH? IS THE SHOW OVER YET?

I ASK YOU TO FREE THE BARD WE CAME TO RESCUE, AND LET US GO HOME TO GAUL BEFORE WE HAVE TO BEAT YOUR ARMY UP AGAIN...

AND I HAVE ONE LAST FAVOUR TO ASK YOU, JULIUS...

YOU SAW THAT? NOT A BAD PROGRAMME, EH?

LEND US CAIUS FATUOUS THE GLADIATOR TRAINER FOR OUR JOURNEY BACK TO GAUL. WE'LL SEND HIM BACK BY RETURN.

GRANTED, BY JUPITER!

BUT... BUT...

WHAT ARE YOU GOING TO DO WITH ME?

WE'RE GOING TO TEACH YOU A LITTLE LESSON, BY BELENOS!

LONG LIVE THE GAULS!

LONG LIVE THE GLADIATORS!

LONG LIVE CAESAR!

WHAT HAPPENED TO ME?

EXACTLY WHAT WILL HAPPEN AGAIN IF YOU DARE SING A NOTE BEFORE WE GET BACK TO GAUL!

NO FEAR! I'M NOT SINGING FOR ANY MORE ROMAN BARBARIANS, AND MOREOVER I'M TAKING NO FURTHER INTEREST IN THE MATTER!

HEY, WHERE ARE THE RUINS? DIDN'T A HOUSE FALL ON ME?

43

AT LAST WE HEAR THE LONG AWAITED SHOUT...

GAUL!!!

HURRAH, BY TOUTATIS!

THANKS FOR THE TRIP, EKONOMIKRISIS. PROMISE TO TAKE THE ROMAN HOME SAFE AND SOUND AND NOT SELL HIM ON THE WAY!

WHAT, SELL A PARTNER?

A FRIEND?

WE'RE VERY FOND OF CAIUS FATUOUS. HE KEEPS US ALL GOING!

RIGHT... OFF WE GO, PARTNER! LET'S SPEED OUR ENTERPRISE ON ITS WAY!

THE GAULISH VILLAGE CELEBRATES THE RETURN OF ITS HEROES WITH A GREAT FEAST... AND BUT FOR THE FACT THAT CACOFONIX WAS THE INVOLUNTARY VICTIM OF A TECHNICAL HITCH, HE WOULD CERTAINLY HAVE GIVEN THEM A SONG...

THE END

GOSCINNY AND UDERZO

PRESENT

An Asterix Adventure

ASTERIX AND THE BANQUET

Written by RENÉ GOSCINNY *and Illustrated by* ALBERT UDERZO

Translated by Anthea Bell *and* Derek Hockridge

PEACE REIGNS IN THE FORTIFIED ROMAN CAMP OF COMPENDIUM...

?!

♪♫

ZZZZ

UNTIL... O CENTURION LOTUSEATUS, THERE'S A VISITOR FROM ROME FOR YOU. LOOKS LIKE TOP BRASS!

HE DOES?

AVE! I AM INSPECTOR GENERAL OVERANXIUS, WITH THE RANK OF PREFECT, ON A SPECIAL MISSION FROM JULIUS CAESAR!

AVE.

ER... PLEASED TO MEET YOU... AND HOW'S CAESAR?

FED TO THE TEETH, BY JUPITER! THAT'S WHY I'M HERE! ALL GAUL IS AT PEACE WITH THE LIBERATING ROMAN ARMY, EXCEPT THIS ONE LITTLE VILLAGE OF DISSIDENTS HERE IN YOUR SECTOR DEFYING THE POWER OF CAESAR!

S... SO?

SO I AM GOING TO LEAD YOUR MEN AGAINST THE VILLAGERS. I'LL SOON GET THEM INTO LINE!

BUT... BUT THOSE GAULS ARE DANGEROUS! THEY HAVE MAGICAL POWERS...

NONSENSE! SOUND THE ASSEMBLY!

WE'RE ENTERING THE LISTS! HOLD THE GAULS AT BAY, AND IT WILL BE ANOTHER BAYLEAF IN CAESAR'S WREATH!*

THE GAULS?!

*WE WOULD SAY: ANOTHER FEATHER IN HIS CAP.

DIRECTLY AFTERWARDS...

SICK BAY

I DIDN'T MEAN THE SICK BAY! WHERE'S YOUR PILUM?

IT MAY BE A BITTER PILUM, BUT WE PREFER THE SICK LISTS.

PEACE REIGNS IN THE GAULISH VILLAGE AS WELL... IT REIGNS TOO HARD FOR THE LIKES OF SOME...

HEY, ASTERIX, THE ROMANS AREN'T ATTACKING US ANY MORE... DO YOU THINK WE'VE ANNOYED THEM?

DON'T LET IT WORRY YOU... WHEN YOU'VE FINISHED DELIVERING MENHIRS, WHY DON'T WE HUNT SOME BOARS?

SOON AFTERWARDS, IN THE FOREST...

SUPPOSE WE WROTE TO THE ROMANS?

WE COULD EXPLAIN THAT...

SSH!

YOU COWARDLY LOT! YOU EXPECT ME TO BELIEVE THAT A HANDFUL OF GAULS COULD RESIST YOU?

DON'T MAKE SO MUCH NOISE, O OVERANXIUS, OR YOU'LL ALERT THE WHOLE HANDFUL!

IT'S THE ROMANS!!!

GOODY!

COME ON, WE MUST TELL THE OTHERS!

MUST WE? WHY NOT JUST DIVIDE THEM BETWEEN US? NO ONE WILL EVER KNOW...

OBELIX, YOU'RE BEING VERY SELFISH! THE OTHERS HAVE A RIGHT TO THEIR BIT OF FUN! ROMANS ARE COMMON PROPERTY.

SO COME ALONG!

IT'S ALWAYS THE SAME! IT'S NOT FAIR, IT JUST ISN'T FAIR... IF THEY WANT ROMANS, WHY CAN'T THEY GO AND FIND SOME OF THEIR OWN...?

A LITTLE LATER...

NOW THEN, NO SHOVING! STAND IN LINE LIKE EVERYONE ELSE!

THERE'S NO NEED TO PUSH... THERE'LL BE PLENTY TO GO ROUND.

ONLY THREE OR FOUR EACH, THAT'S ALL... WILL YOU LEND ME YOURS, ASTERIX?

COME ON, WHAT ARE YOU WAITING FOR? CHARGE, MEN! CHARGE!

MUMMY!

O CHIEF VITALSTATISTIX, THE ROMANS ARE PUTTING UP A STOCKADE ALL ROUND THE VILLAGE!

GOODNESS ME, WHAT FOR? LET'S TAKE A LOOK...

THESE ROMANS ARE CRAZY!

SINCE YOU'RE SO CLEVER, BY MINERVA, I'M SHUTTING YOU UP IN YOUR VILLAGE! YOU WON'T BE ABLE TO GO SPREADING YOUR SEDITIOUS OPINIONS THROUGH GAUL!

YOU'LL HAVE TO BE SELF-SUFFICIENT AND LIVE ON THE PRODUCE OF YOUR OWN VILLAGE! THE OUTSIDE WORLD WILL FORGET YOU!

GAUL IS OUR COUNTRY, O ROMAN, AND WE'LL GO WHERE WE LIKE IN IT...

I'LL MAKE A BET WITH YOU: WE SHALL GET OUT OF OUR VILLAGE IN SPITE OF YOUR STOCKADE AND YOUR LEGIONARIES, AND WE'LL GO ON A TOUR OF GAUL...

...BRINGING BACK ALL ITS REGIONAL SPECIALITIES! ON OUR RETURN, WE'LL INVITE YOU TO A BANQUET TO PROVE WE ARE TELLING THE TRUTH!

HARGH HARGH GNGNGNGN!!

DONE, O GAULS! IF YOU WIN YOUR BET I WILL RAISE THE SIEGE AND GO BACK TO ROME TO TELL JULIUS CAESAR I'VE FAILED!

AND WHEN YOU GET THERE, GIVE OUR REGARDS TO OUR OLD FRIEND CAIUS FATUOUS.

KEEP AN EYE ON THEM!

AN EYE IT'LL HAVE TO BE... I CAN'T OPEN THE OTHER ONE YET!

* SEE ASTERIX AND THE GOLDEN SICKLE

WE NEED SOME MEANS OF TRANSPORT...

USED CHARIOTS

AFTER A NICE CHARIOT, GENTLEMEN? I'VE GOT A SPECIAL UNREPEATABLE OFFER HERE!

NEARLY NEW, ONE MATRON DRIVER, HARDLY ANY MILEAGE! SEE THE SHINE ON THAT HORSE'S COAT! SEE THAT CHASSIS! THE CARRIAGEWORK! THIS CHARIOT'S HARDLY BEEN RUN IN! A GOLDEN OPPORTUNITY!

RIGHT, WE'RE IN A HURRY. WE'LL TAKE IT.

YOU WON'T REGRET YOUR BARGAIN...

ONCE OUTSIDE LUTETIA...

AND IT'S RAINING...

GOOD-LOOKING HORSE, BUT NOT VERY FAST...

OUR HORSE SEEMS A BIT OFF COLOUR!

THERE GOES A WHEEL!

CLANG!

YOU KNOW, ASTERIX, I THINK WE'VE BEEN HAD!

WE'RE IN LUCK... HERE COMES A BREAKDOWN CHARIOT!

BREAKDOWNS

70

BETTER GET OUT BEFORE THE OTHER ONE COMES BACK!

YOOHOO! ASTERIX! HERE I AM!

!!!

LOOK WHAT I FOUND, ASTERIX! I'LL LET YOU HAVE A LITTLE IF YOU LIKE.

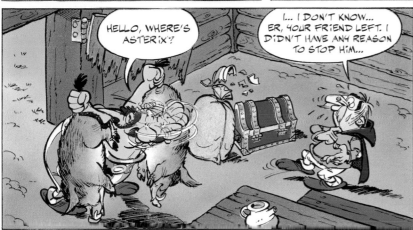

HELLO, WHERE'S ASTERIX?

I... I DON'T KNOW... ER, YOUR FRIEND LEFT. I DIDN'T HAVE ANY REASON TO STOP HIM...

ASTERIX WOULD NEVER HAVE LEFT WITHOUT ME! WHERE IS HE?

MERCY! I'LL TALK!

I ... I'M A MISFIT, YOU SEE, IT'S ALL BECAUSE OF MY UNDERPRIVILEGED ENVIRONMENTAL SITUATION, AND I BETRAYED ASTERIX TO THE ROMANS WHO TOOK HIM TO THE NEAREST GARRISON TOWN...

WHAT'S THIS TOWN CALLED?

DIVODURUM.

I DON'T CARE IF YOU'VE ORDERED RUM OR NOT. YOU DON'T SOFTEN ME UP LIKE THAT! WHERE'S ASTERIX?

IN DIVODURUM.* IT'S THE NAME OF THE TOWN. IT'S EAST OF HERE.

* METZ...

I'LL NEVER BETRAY MY FELLOW-COUNTRYMEN AGAIN. THE PAY'S GOOD, BUT IT'S DANGEROUS WORK...

...AND MORALLY INDEFENSIBLE.

77

HERE WE ARE... A GARRISON TOWN, HE SAID...

DIVODURUM

ASTERIX MUST HAVE BEEN TAKEN TO PRISON. NOW THE BEST WAY TO FIND THE PRISON AND GET INSIDE WOULD BE TO GET TAKEN TO PRISON MYSELF...

SO AS SOON AS I SEE A LEGIONARY I'LL SLAP HIS FACE AND HE'LL CART ME OFF TO PRISON... AH, HERE COMES A GOOD ONE!

PAF!

WELL, COME ON, THEN! PUT ME IN IRONS, CAN'T YOU? TAKE ME TO PRISON!

HEY, TAKE ME TO PRISON! I'VE KNOCKED OUT A LEGIONARY!

QUICK, LEAVE THE LEGIONARY THERE AND HIDE, OR THE ROMANS WILL TAKE YOU PRISONER!

BUT I WANT THEM TO TAKE ME PRISONER! I'M LOOKING FOR THE PRISON!

YOU ARE? WELL, IF YOU'RE SURE YOU WANT THE PRISON, TAKE THE THIRD TURNING ON THE RIGHT.

THANKS.

THIS IS YOURS. I KNOCKED HIM OUT. CAN I COME IN?

?!??

OBELIX!

ASTERIX! AT LAST! I'VE HAD TROUBLE FINDING YOU. COME ON, LET'S GO.

GIVE ME SOME POTION TO DRINK. THE GOURD'S ON MY BELT.

RIGHT.

GLUG!
GLUG!
GLUG!

I SOMETIMES WONDER IF WE COULD GO INTO BUSINESS WITH THE POTION... BUT IT MIGHT BE A DRUG ON THE MARKET.

CLANG!

LET'S GO!

NO! LEAVE THAT DOOR ALONE!

YOU'VE GOT NO RIGHT TO...

OUCH!

CRASH!

WOULD YOU MIND...

WHAT ON EARTH IS GOING ON IN THERE?

TCHAFF!

OH, I'VE GONE AND LEFT THE SHOPPING BAG IN OUR CELL. I'LL HAVE TO GO BACK FOR IT!

TALK ABOUT ABSENT-MINDED. HURRY UP!

WATCH OUT! HE'S COMING BACK!

MIND THAT DOOR!

OUCH!

CRASH!

CAN'T YOU LEAVE US IN PEACE?

HERE WE ARE!

IT'S TOO LATE TO BUY ANYTHING FOR THE BANQUET HERE. WE'LL MAKE UP FOR IT AT OUR NEXT STOP, LUGDUNUM.*

* LYONS

IS LUGDUNUM FAR?

YES, WE'LL NEED TRANSPORT.

POST HOUSE

79

I'M JELLIBABIX, HEAD OF THE RESISTANCE MOVEMENT HERE. YOU'RE FELLOW GAULS, AND WE KNOW ABOUT YOUR BET. WE'LL HELP YOU BY PUTTING THE ROMAN GARRISON OUT OF ACTION FOR A FEW HOURS...

HOW CAN YOU DO THAT?

LUGDUNUM HAS ANY AMOUNT OF ALLEYWAYS, A POSITIVE MAZE OF THEM, WHERE THE ROMANS HESITATE TO VENTURE... WELL, WE'LL LURE THEM IN!

WAIT FOR ME HERE!

WHAT DO YOU WANT, GAUL?

TO SEE THE PREFECT. I HAVE IMPORTANT INFORMATION.

YOU KNOW WHERE THE TWO OUTLAWS ARE? EXCELLENT! YOU CAN GUIDE MY WHOLE GARRISON!

SOON AFTERWARDS

CAESAR WILL REWARD ME WELL FOR THIS!

?!

HEY, WAIT A MINUTE!!

BY VULCAN, WHERE ARE YOU, GAUL?!

HERE!

?!?

HERE!

HERE!

HERE!

HERE!

HERE!

THEY'RE TRYING TO GET US LOST... LET'S RETRACE OUR STEPS!

AND SOON...

YOOHOO! ARE YOU THERE FIBROSITUS?

NO, I'M HERE!

I DON'T KNOW WHERE I AM!

JUST OUTSIDE THE MAZE...

THOSE WRETCHED GAULS ARE TRYING TO FOOL ME... I'M GOING IN TO LOOK FOR MY GARRISON!

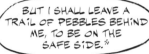

BUT I SHALL LEAVE A TRAIL OF PEBBLES BEHIND ME, TO BE ON THE SAFE SIDE.*

* AN IDEA LATER TAKEN UP BY A FAMOUS TELLER OF FAIRY TALES, WHICH GOES TO SHOW THAT IMITATION IS THE SINCEREST FORM OF FLATTERY.

HEY, GARRISON, WHERE ARE YOU?

ON THE OTHER SIDE OF TOWN...

IT'LL TAKE THE ROMANS ALL DAY TO GET OUT... YOU CAN CARRY ON WITH YOUR JOURNEY. WE'VE GOT YOU A CHARIOT.

THE THING IS...

WE HAVE TO BUY SOMETHING FOR OUR BANQUET... THE LOCAL SPECIALITIES OF LUGDUNUM.

WE THOUGHT OF THAT. HERE: SAUSAGE AND MEAT-BALLS.

HOW CAN WE THANK YOU?

BY WINNING YOUR BET, FRIENDS!

YOOHOO! ARE YOU THERE?

OH, WAS IT YOU WHO DROPPED ALL THOSE PEBBLES, O PREFECT POISONUS FUNGUS? HERE, I'VE BEEN PICKING THEM UP FOR YOU!

I WANT TO GET OUT OF HERE, DECURION!

NOW LET'S ALL KEEP CALM! DON'T PANIC!

6-63

93

NOW, FULL SPEED AHEAD TO OUR NEXT PORT OF CALL, NICAE!*

*NICE

CRACK!

ROMAN ROAD VII, THAT'LL BE IT!

VR VII

?!?

GET A MOVE ON!

GET A MOVE ON WHERE, EH, GRANDPA?

IF I'D ONLY KNOWN...

IF IFS AND ANDS WERE CAULDRONS AND AMPHORAS...

WATCH OUT! YOU'LL RAM MY OXEN!

SERVICE BH STATION
BEST HAY
I MILIA PASSUUM

WHAT'S GOING ON HERE?

DON'T YOU KNOW? THIS IS THE START OF THE SUMMER HOLIDAY, AND EVERYONE'S GOING SOUTH TO THE SEASIDE FOR PEACE AND QUIET!

GET OUT OF THAT CART IF YOU'RE A MAN!

I'VE BEEN IN THE ARMY, I HAVE! I'D HAVE YOU KNOW I FOUGHT WITH VERCINGETORIX AT GERGOVIA!

CALL THIS PEACE AND QUIET?

THESE LUTETIANS ARE CRAZY!

AN INN! LET'S STOP FOR A BITE AND A LITTLE REAL PEACE!

GOOD IDEA.

I ORDERED BOAR. THIS IS VEAL!

BOAR'S OFF, AND IF YOU DON'T WANT THAT VEAL THERE ARE PLENTY OF PEOPLE WAITING WHO DO!

FINALLY THE ROAD WINDS PAST OLIVE TREES...

THESE NORTHERNERS ARE CRAZY!

THAT DOES IT! HE GRAZED MY WING!

WELL, WHY DIDN'T YOU TAKE YOUR HELMET OFF THEN, GRANDPA?

24

85

THIS IS WHAT WE NEED!

NO! NO! I HIRED THIS BOAT FOR MYSELF! YOU'LL CAPSIZE IT!

WE'RE GOING OUT TO SEA! THIS IS MOST UNWISE! WHERE ARE YOU GOING?

MASSILIA.

FAT, INDEED! I'VE GOT A POWERFUL PHYSIQUE, THAT'S ALL.

BUT I DON'T WANT TO GO TO MASSILIA! I HAD A LOT OF TROUBLE FINDING A ROOM WITH FULL BOARD IN NICAE, AND I DON'T WANT TO MISS LUNCH!

WELL, THIS IS A BOARDING PARTY BOUND FOR MASSILIA, SO YOUR LUNCH WILL HAVE TO GO BY THE BOARD!

ANYWAY IT'S ALL MUSCLE. NOT AN OUNCE OF FAT, JUST MUSCLE!

AT LAST, AFTER A LONG SEA JOURNEY, OUR FRIENDS TIE UP AT THE GREAT PORT OF MASSILIA...

THANKS FOR THE BOAT RIDE.

I THOUGHT IT WAS US TAKING HIM FOR A RIDE, ASTERIX?

HEY, YOU! WHERE ARE YOU TAKING THAT BOAT?

BACK TO NICAE. I'VE GOT A ROOM THERE, WITH FULL BOARD.

GOING BACK TO NICAE BY SEA? WHAT, WITH THE MISTRAL COMING UP? VESUVIUS ERUPTING IS NOTHING TO IT! ARE YOU CRAZY?

THIS IS THE LAST TIME I EVER GO TO THE SOUTH OF GAUL ON HOLIDAY!

TOUCH OF THE SUN, EH? THESE LUTETIANS ARE CRAZY!

86

DRINKLIKAFIX
TUNAFIX

LET'S GO IN FOR A BITE AND A SUP AND A LITTLE INFORMATION.

HEY, CÉSAR! COMPANY!

CAESAR?!

NO, NOT THAT ONE! I'M NOT JULIUS CAESAR, I'M CÉSAR DRINKLIKAFIX, LANDLORD OF THIS INN.

PLEASED TO MEET YOU... CAN YOU TELL US WHERE WE CAN BUY SOME FISH STEW TO TAKE AWAY?

FISH STEW?

HEY, HYDROPHOBIA! GET SOME FISH STEW COOKING!

HAVE A PASTIX?

NO THANKS, WE'D RATHER HAVE GOAT'S MILK...

AND A BOAR, IF YOU'VE GOT ONE...

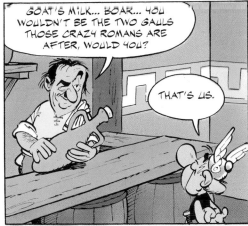

GOAT'S MILK... BOAR... YOU WOULDN'T BE THE TWO GAULS THOSE CRAZY ROMANS ARE AFTER, WOULD YOU?

THAT'S US.

THEN WELCOME TO MASSILIA! DRINKS ALL ROUND ON ME! MILK FOR YOU, PASTIX FOR US!

NOT FOR ME, THANKS...

WHEN I OFFER DRINKS ON THE HOUSE, SIR, PEOPLE DRINK THEM, IF THEY DON'T WANT TO SEEM LIKE A FISH OUT OF WATER!

27

87

HURRY UP, OBELIX. I'D LIKE TO GET TO TOLOSA* AS SOON AS WE CAN.

IT'S NEARLY DARK...

*TOULOUSE

THERE YOU ARE, WHAT DID I SAY? CAN'T SEE A THING.

WELL, LET'S STOP HERE FOR THE NIGHT, OBELIX. WE CAN GO ON IN THE MORNING.

GOOD NIGHT, ASTERIX.

GOOD NIGHT, OBELIX.

TANTAN TARAA! TARAA

?!?

ARE THOSE NEW RECRUITS?

NO! IT'S THE TWO GAULS!!

WE'VE SPENT THE NIGHT IN THE MIDDLE OF A ROMAN CAMP!

WHAT LUCK!

QUICK! GET THEM! WE'LL TAKE THEM TO PREFECT ADIPUS AT TOLOSA!

THERE ARE QUITE A LOT OF THEM. I'LL JUST TAKE A DROP OF MAGIC POTION...

MIND IF I START WITHOUT YOU, ASTERIX?

GET THEEEEEE...

PAF!

AND A FEW MINUTES AFTER THE TRUMPET HAS BLOWN REVEILLE...

I'VE BEEN THINKING, OBELIX... THAT ROMAN WANTED TO TAKE US TO TOLOSA. IT WOULDN'T BE A BAD IDEA TO LET THE ROMANS GIVE US TRANSPORT, WOULD IT?

NO... BUT WE'LL HAVE TO WAIT A BIT BEFORE WE CAN SUGGEST IT...

TH... THANKS.

DON'T MENTION IT.

THERE... THAT'S DONE.

RIGHT, NOW GO AND PUT MY FRIEND BACK IN CHAINS. WE'RE WASTING TIME!

STOP TREMBLING LIKE THAT, OR YOU'LL NEVER GET THE JOB DONE!

SNAP!

I'LL GIVE YOU A HAND, OR WE'LL BE HERE ALL DAY.

?!?

STOP IT, WILL YOU? STOP IT!!!

AND AT LAST...

THERE, CENTURION, THAT'S DONE. AVE.

JUST A MOMENT! WE FORGOT OUR SHOPPING BAG. IT'S OVER THERE!

SNAP!

DON'T WORRY, ASTERIX. I'LL GET IT.

SNAP!

BOOHOOHOO!

NOW, NOW, CALM DOWN. NEVER MIND, WE'LL PUT THEM IN THE CART WITHOUT CHAINING THEM UP!

SEE? THIS WAY WE'LL GET TO TOLOSA WITHOUT ANY TROUBLE. AND THE FUNNY THING IS WE'RE THE PRISONERS AND THEY'RE THE ONES TRUDGING ALONG ON FOOT!

THESE ROMANS ARE CRAZY!

AND AFTER A LONG, PEACEFUL JOURNEY...

WE'RE IN SIGHT OF TOLOSA. WAIT FOR ME HERE. I'M OFF TO TELL THE PREFECT WE'VE ARRIVED.

91

AFTER THIS GREAT VICTORY OF MINE I'M SURE TO GET AN ADMINISTRATIVE POST IN ROME.

TOLOSA

I WANT TO SEE THE PREFECT AT ONCE! IT'S IMPORTANT.

WELL, CENTURION? YOU HAVE NEWS FOR ME?

YES, O PREFECT ADIPUS. I'D LIKE YOU TO COME TO THE OUTSKIRTS OF TOLOSA. I HAVE A LITTLE SURPRISE FOR YOU!

SOON AFTERWARDS

I LIKE SURPRISES, AND THE EXERCISE WILL DO ME GOOD.

NEARLY THERE. THIS WILL BE QUITE A SURPRISE!

BY JUPITER!

THE PRISONERS! WHERE ARE THE PRISONERS?

THIS IS YOUR SURPRISE? A SET OF SEMI-CONSCIOUS LEGIONARIES?

THEY WENT OFF SOON AFTER YOU LEFT... THEY SAID THEY HADN'T COME TO TOLOSA TO SEE ANY PREFECT, THEY WANTED SOME OF THE LOCAL SAUSAGE.

SAUSAGE? PREFECT? WHAT ON EARTH IS ALL THIS ABOUT, BY MINERVA?

NOTHING! NOTHING! FORGET IT!

SOBS

MEANWHILE OUR FRIENDS ARE LEAVING TOLOSA...

PRETTY PLACE, TOLOSA.... IS THE SAUSAGE NICE?

SNIFF! SNIFF!

DELICIOUS, OBELIX!

ALL OVER GAUL, THE INFURIATED ROMANS ARE PUTTING UP POSTERS OFFERING A REWARD FOR THE CAPTURE OF OUR FRIENDS...

50,000 SESTERTII REWARD FOR INFORMATION LEADING TO THE ARREST OF

ASTERIX & OBELIX
THE TWO DANGEROUS OUTLAWS

AND IN THE TOWN OF AGINUM*...

* AGEN

GOOD FOR THEM!

YOU COULDN'T CALL THEM HANDSOME, BUT THEY HAVE CHARISMA!

I WONDER IF THEY'LL BE STOPPING HERE ON THEIR TOUR OF GAUL?

I'M SURE THEY WILL. THEY'LL WANT TO BUY OUR FAMOUS PRUNES. I HEARD THEY'VE BEEN SEEN IN TOLOSA!

50,000 SESTERTII REWARD FOR INFORMATION LEADING TO THE ARREST OF

ASTERIX & OBELIX
THE TWO DANGEROUS OUTLAWS

IN THE ROMAN GARRISON COMMANDER'S OFFICE...

THESE TWO GAULS ARE VERY STRONG. I'VE THOUGHT OF A CUNNING STRATAGEM...

I'LL GIVE THEM DRUGGED FOOD TO EAT, THEY WILL FALL ASLEEP, AND ALL YOU HAVE TO DO IS PICK THEM UP FROM MY INN.

NOT THE KIND OF THING I REALLY LIKE, BUT ALL RIGHT, UPTOTRIX.

NOT A MOMENT TO LOSE! I MUST GO AND MEET THEM!

THEY'RE COMING! THEY'RE COMING!

ASTERIX AND OBELIX'S TOUR OF GAUL IS MORE LIKE A ROMAN TRIUMPH...

THREE CHEERS!

VERY NICE OF THEM, BUT THE ROMANS MIGHT NOTICE SOMETHING...

KEEP GOING!

WAIT A MINUTE, FRIENDS! YOU ARE NATIONAL HEROES... WOULD YOU DO ME THE HONOUR OF TAKING REFRESHMENT AT MY HUMBLE INN?

?!?

MY NAME IS UPTOTRIX. I CAN OFFER YOU PRUNES AND WILD BOAR!

LET'S BE CAREFUL, OBELIX. WE'VE ALREADY BEEN BETRAYED ONCE.

BOAR! OH, COME ON ASTERIX!

94

MUST BE NICE TO BE ABLE TO DROP OFF SO EASILY!

LET'S GET OUT OF HERE. THE ROMANS CAN WAKE UP MINE HOST!

ZZZZ ZZZZ!

WE CAN MOVE MORE FREELY WITHOUT THE CART... BUT YOU'D BETTER GIVE ME THE BAG. THE POOR HORSE CAN'T CARRY THE WEIGHT AS WELL AS YOURS.

MY WEIGHT? WHAT ABOUT MY WEIGHT?

IT'S TOO HEAVY, THAT'S WHAT ABOUT YOUR WEIGHT! HAND ME THAT BAG AND DON'T BE SO PIG-HEADED!

OH YES, MISTER ASTERIX ALWAYS GIVES THE ORDERS! MISTER ASTERIX IS THE BOSS! MISTER ASTERIX IS ALWAYS RIGHT!

WELL, IF THE HORSE CAN'T CARRY ME AND THE BAG, THEN WE'LL CARRY THE HORSE.

PROLONGED SULKS

THERE, WHAT DID I SAY?

?

PLOF!

NO SUCH THING! THAT WAS A LONG LAP AND HE'S TIRED, THAT'S ALL!

YOU KNOW THAT WASN'T IT, OBELIX, BUT YOU'RE RIGHT, IT WAS A LONG LAP! LET'S STOP HERE FOR SOME SLEEP.

IN THE NIGHT...

RRRR RRRR

ZZZZ

TRAVELLERS! LET'S STEAL THEIR LUGGAGE!

YEAH!

NEWS OF THE SENSATIONAL CAPTURE HAS REACHED THE TOWN OF BURDIGALA*...

WHAT A SHAME!

OUR POOR FELLOW-COUNTRYMEN!

TO FAIL AT THIS STAGE!

IF ONLY WE COULD HELP THEM!

* BORDEAUX

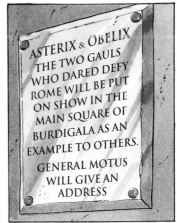

ASTERIX & OBELIX
THE TWO GAULS WHO DARED DEFY ROME WILL BE PUT ON SHOW IN THE MAIN SQUARE OF BURDIGALA AS AN EXAMPLE TO OTHERS.

GENERAL MOTUS WILL GIVE AN ADDRESS

...AND THIS BAG OF FOOD, DESTINED FOR THE GAULISH BANQUET, IS PROOF POSITIVE THAT THESE TWO NOTORIOUS OUTLAWS, WHO DARED DEFY THE MIGHT OF ROME, HAVE FAILED IN THEIR ATTEMPT!

BUT I TELL YOU WE'RE VILLANUS...

...AND UNSCRUPULUS!

THEY'RE TELLING THE TRUTH!

?!

AND WE'D LIKE OUR SHOPPING BAG BACK. WE'RE IN A HURRY.

ASTERIX AND OBELIX!
THREE CHEERS!

COME ON, LADS HELP THEM!

OUR HEROES!

LEGIONARIES! SEIZE THOSE MEN!

* HENCE THE EXPRESSION: A DIPLOMATIC BAG

LET'S MAKE FOR THE HARBOUR. WE'LL SEE IF WE CAN BOARD A SHIP FOR HOME...

HURRY UP UNLOADING, YOU LAZY LOT, OR I'LL MISS THE TIDE!

MENHIRS!

YOU'RE FROM ARMORICA?

YES, CAPTAIN SENIORSERVIX, FROM GESOCRIBATUM.* I'M GOING BACK TO ARMORICA AS SOON AS MY CARGO'S UNLOADED.

* LE CONQUET

CAN WE COME WITH YOU?

I'LL SEE TO YOUR MENHIRS. I KNOW HOW TO HANDLE MENHIRS!

SEE?

?!?

AND SOON

I THINK THAT'S THE LOT!

WHY, YOU MUST BE ASTERIX AND OBELIX! IT WILL BE AN HONOUR TO HAVE YOU ON BOARD MY SHIP!

THANK YOU, CAPTAIN!

AND...

CAST OFF THERE!

HEY! THERE SHOULD BE 39 ARTICLES! I'M STILL 4 SHORT. YOU'VE GOT MY ORDERS WRONG!

SORRY... ANOTHER MENHIR COMING OVER. CATCH!

BOF!

...STILL 3 SHORT, AND I'M FORESHORTENED! THIS GAME'S NOT WORTH THE CANDLE!

39

YOU TWO, STEP OUT...

PHEW! I WAS GETTING HOT IN THERE!

...OF LINE!

?!?

?

COME ON, OBELIX, AND DON'T FORGET THE SHOPPING BAG!

GIVE ME COVER, MEN! I'M GOING TO ARREST THEM!

ALARM IS DULY RAISED, AND THE HARBOUR OF GESOCRIBATUM ECHOES TO THE SOUND OF CONTRADICTORY ORDERS...

ALL HANDS ON SHORE!

CAST OFF THERE!

NO, DON'T! WE'RE JUST COMING ON SHORE!

WHAT EXACTLY IS GOING ON?

DON'T ASK ME. WHEN IT COMES TO CURRENT EVENTS I'M NEVER IN THE SWIM!

RAISE THE ALARM! RAISE THE ALARM!!

R. GOSCINNY · ASTERIX · A. UDERZO

Asterix and CLEOPATRA

Written by René GOSCINNY   Illustrated by Albert UDERZO

GOSCINNY AND UDERZO
PRESENT
An Asterix Adventure

ASTERIX
AND
CLEOPATRA

Written by RENÉ GOSCINNY *and Illustrated by* ALBERT UDERZO

Translated by Anthea Bell *and* Derek Hockridge

ALEXANDRIA, CAPITAL OF EGYPT. THE PALACE OF THE FABULOUS QUEEN CLEOPATRA, OF WHOM IT WAS SAID THAT IF HER NOSE HAD BEEN SHORTER IT WOULD HAVE CHANGED THE WHOLE COURSE OF HISTORY...

THAT'S AN INFAMOUS SUGGESTION, O CAESAR!

YOU HAVE TO FACE FACTS, O QUEEN! YOURS IS A DECADENT NATION, ONLY FIT TO LIVE IN SEMI-SLAVERY UNDER THE ROMANS.

MY PEOPLE BUILT THE PYRAMIDS! THE TOWER OF PHAROS! THE TEMPLES – THE OBELISKS!

THAT'S OLD HAT! ALL THEY CAN DO NOW IS WAIT FOR THE ANNUAL FLOODING OF THE NILE!

THAT WILL DO!

CRASH!

I, CLEOPATRA, WILL PROVE TO YOU, O CAESAR, THAT MY PEOPLE ARE AS BRILLIANT AS EVER! IN THREE MONTHS' TIME I'LL HAVE A MAGNIFICENT PALACE BUILT HERE FOR YOU IN ALEXANDRIA!

WELL, IF YOU CAN DO THAT, O QUEEN, I'LL ADMIT THAT THE EGYPTIANS ARE STILL A GREAT NATION...

...BUT I HAVE MY DOUBTS!

SHE'S A NICE GIRL, ONLY HER NOSE IS SO EASILY PUT OUT OF JOINT...

CRASH!

...PRETTY NOSE TOO!

SOON AFTERWARDS...

N.B. FOR THE CONVENIENCE OF OUR READERS, WE GIVE A DUBBED VERSION OF THE ORIGINAL DIALOGUE...

EDIFIS, I HAVE SUMMONED YOU BECAUSE YOU ARE THE BEST ARCHITECT IN ALEXANDRIA ...WHICH ISN'T SAYING MUCH.

OH!*

* OWING TO THE FACT THAT DUBBING TECHNIQUES HAD NOT BEEN PERFECTED AT THIS PERIOD, THE MOVEMENT OF THE LIPS DOES NOT SYNCHRONIZE VERY WELL WITH THE WORDS.

DON'T ANSWER BACK! YOUR BUILDINGS ARE FLIMSY! YOU CAN HEAR EVERY WORD THE NEIGHBOURS SAY! THE CEILINGS FALL IN!

IT'S THESE MODERN MATERIALS... ACTUALLY, WHAT I REALLY WANT TO DO IS BUILD PYRAMIDS AND...

SILENCE! YOU HAVE JUST THREE MONTHS TO MAKE GOOD. YOU ARE TO BUILD JULIUS CAESAR A MAGNIFICENT PALACE HERE IN ALEXANDRIA.

DID YOU SAY **THREE MONTHS?**

IF YOU SUCCEED I WILL COVER YOU WITH GOLD! IF NOT, YOU'LL BE THROWN TO THE CROCODILES! YOU MAY GO!

THREE MONTHS! I'D NEED SUPERNATURAL POWERS TO DO THAT! I'D NEED SOMEONE WHO CAN WORK MAGIC...

GOT IT! I KNOW THE VERY MAN! HE CAN WORK MAGIC!

AND FAR AWAY, IN A LITTLE VILLAGE IN GAUL...

VI, VI, VI* AGAIN, IT'S LIKE MAGIC!

HA! HA! IT **IS** MAGIC!

THIS ROMAN GAME WILL NEVER CATCH ON...

* 3 SIXES

PEACE REIGNS IN THE VILLAGE OF THE INDOMITABLE GAULS, BUT IT IS SOON TO BE DISTURBED...

I'M GOING TO TRAIN THIS LITTLE DOG TO CARRY MENHIRS!

ARE YOU? MEANWHILE, WHY NOT LAY THE TABLE FOR US TO EAT THIS BIG BOAR?

...BY THE ARRIVAL OF A STRANGE STRANGER...

COULD YOU TELL ME WHERE TO FIND GETAFIX THE DRUID, PLEASE?

UP THAT TREE, PICKING MISTLETOE.

GETAFIX?

WHAT A DELIGHTFUL SURPRISE!

?!

MY DEAR OLD GETAFIX, I HOPE I FIND YOU WELL?

AN ALEXANDRINE...

MEET MY FRIEND EDIFIS FROM ALEXANDRIA! HE'S AN ARCHITECT. I GOT TO KNOW HIM ON MY TRAVELS.

GETAFIX, I'VE COME ALL THIS WAY BECAUSE I NEED YOUR HELP...

I HAVE TO BUILD CAESAR A PALACE WITHIN THREE MONTHS. IF I DON'T CLEOPATRA WILL THROW ME TO THE CROCODILES...

...AND UNLESS YOU USE YOUR MAGIC POWERS TO HELP ME I'LL NEVER DO IT! BOOHOO!

ARE CROCODILES NICE TO EAT?

SHUT UP, OBELIX!

DON'T WORRY, EDIFIS! IT SO HAPPENS I WANTED TO GO TO ALEXANDRIA TO LOOK A FEW THINGS UP IN THE LIBRARY THERE...

THIS IS MY CHANCE! I'LL GO BACK TO EGYPT WITH YOU.

US TOO!

BY OSIRIS! WILL YOU REALLY?

WOOF! WOOF!

111

MY SHIP IS WAITING OFFSHORE.

JUST GIVE US TIME TO PACK AND SAY GOODBYE, AND WE'LL BE WITH YOU!

COME ALONG, DOGMATIX, WE'RE GOING ON A NICE SEA VOYAGE!

YOU'RE NEVER GOING TO TAKE HIM?

AND WHY NOT, MAY I ASK, MR ASTERIX?

BECAUSE HE'S TOO SMALL FOR SUCH A LONG JOURNEY, THAT'S WHY NOT, MR OBELIX!

WHAT'S MORE, THERE ARE CATS IN EGYPT! NO, NOT ANOTHER WORD! YOU GO AND PACK.

IT'S ALWAYS THE SAME! I'M JUST AN EXTRA! A MAKEWEIGHT! NO ONE EVER LISTENS TO ME!

SOON AFTERWARDS

YOU, MY FRIENDS, ARE TO REPRESENT THE SPIRIT OF GAUL ON THE BANKS OF THE NILE! SHOW YOURSELVES TRUE BORN GAULS, BY TOUTATIS, AND MAY THE SKY NEVER FALL ON YOUR HEADS!

HEY!

GOODBYE, THEN, AND THANKS, CHIEF VITALSTATISTIX!

HEY!

EH?

NO, CACOFONIX, YOU ARE NOT, REPEAT NOT, GOING TO SING!!!

BOING! BOING! BOING!

BUT I WASN'T GOING TO SING! I ONLY WANTED TO TELL HIM HE WAS TREADING ON MY TOE!

SOON AFTERWARDS...

WOOF!

?

JUST ME BARKING! I CAN BARK, CAN'T I, EVEN IF I'M NOT ALLOWED TO TALK?

ALL RIGHT, YOU WIN, YOU PIGHEADED GREAT IDIOT! LET HIM OUT!

THERE'S MY SHIP, THE NASTIUPSET.

WE CAN CAST OFF NOW, SETHISBACKUP?

HONESTLY, ASTERIX, I SWEAR I DON'T KNOW HOW HE GOT INTO MY BAG!

NO, NO, OF COURSE NOT! HURRY UP OR WE'LL MISS THE TIDE.

AND WITH AN ICY WINTER WIND BEHIND THEM, OUR FRIENDS SET SAIL ON THEIR LONG VOYAGE TO EGYPT AND THE FABULOUS CLEOPATRA...

IN EGYPT WE SHALL HAVE TO CONTEND WITH LABOUR TROUBLES, THE TIME FACTOR, THE ROMANS, WHO WON'T WANT US TO WIN CLEOPATRA'S BET...

AND ABOVE ALL WITH ARTIFIS, A RIVAL ARCHITECT. HE'S ALWAYS GOT IT IN FOR ME. HE HAS A LOT OF TALENTS...

CLEVER, IS HE?

NO, RICH. HE HAS A LOT OF GOLD TALENTS – THAT'S THE MONEY WE USE IN EGYPT.

AND THEN THERE'S ALWAYS THE DANGER OF PIRATES ON THE WAY.

OH, WE'LL TAKE CARE OF THAT! RIGHT, OBELIX?

SURE ENOUGH, NOT FAR AWAY...

RIGHT, BOYS! WE'RE STEERING CLEAR OF ALL GAULS THIS TIME! AVOID ROMAN AND PHOENICIAN VESSELS TOO – THEY SOMETIMES USE THOSE. I'M PLAYING SAFE... I HAD TO LEAVE MY SON ERIX ON DEPOSIT TO BUY THIS SHIP!

NEXT INSTALMENT COMING UP, SIR! EGYPTIAN SHIP TO STARBOARD.

SPLENDID! WE'LL MAKE OUR FORTUNES! WE'LL DO IT YET! GET READY TO BOARD HER!

WHAT'S THE LOOKOUT SAYING?

HE SAYS THERE'S A PIRATE SHIP TO PORT.

HONEST? YOU'RE NOT JOKING?

IT'S THEM, ASTERIX, IT'S THEM! YOOHOO! YOOHOO! COMING!

IT ISN'T TRUE! IT **CAN'T** BE TRUE! IT'S THEM! GET OUT OF HERE, FAST! QUICK, SCUTTLE!

TOO LATE, CAP'N! THEY'RE SCUTTLING FASTER!

SCUTTLE THE SHIP, I MEAN! SAVES US A FEW KNOCKS, AND COMES TO THE SAME THING IN THE END.

SOON AFTERWARDS...

WELL, YOU SAID WE'D DO IT, AND HERE WE ARE, DONE! ALEA JACTA EST!

ONE MORE CLASSICAL REMARK FROM YOU AND I'LL MAKE YOU EAT YOUR WOODEN LEG!

OFFSIDE! FOUL! UNSPORTING!

AMAZING! THOSE PIRATES TOOK ONE LOOK AT YOU AND SANK THEIR OWN SHIP RATHER THAN FIGHT!

OH, WE'RE OLD FRIENDS... WE OFTEN GO SAILING TOGETHER.

ONE NIGHT, AFTER A LONG, PEACEFUL VOYAGE...

WHAT'S THAT LIGHT ON THE HORIZON, EDIFIS?

IT'S THE TOWER OF PHAROS, ASTERIX. ITS LIGHT GUIDES SHIPS INTO THE HARBOUR...

WE'LL REACH ALEXANDRIA TOMORROW.

A TOWER TO GUIDE SHIPS? THESE EGYPTIANS ARE CRAZY!

THIS, MY DEAR OBELIX, IS ONE OF THE SEVEN WONDERS OF THE WORLD!

NEXT MORNING...

AS SOON AS WE LAND I'LL TAKE YOU TO THE PALACE TO MEET THE QUEEN.

AND IN HER PALACE THE LUXURY-LOVING CLEOPATRA IS SITTING DOWN TO HER FAVOURITE SNACK – PEARLS DISSOLVED IN VINEGAR.

WHERE ARE THE PEARL TONGS, FOR OSIRIS'S SAKE?

HERE, TASTER! GET ON WITH YOUR JOB!

VERY WELL, O QUEEN!

THE GREEDY PIG! SHE'S TAKEN FOUR PEARLS AGAIN!

UGH! I DO HATE TOO MUCH PEARL IN MY VINEGAR!

EDIFIS THE ARCHITECT CRAVES THE HONOUR OF AN AUDIENCE!

SHOW HIM IN...

MEET MY FRIENDS FROM GAUL, O QUEEN – A POWERFUL MAGICIAN AND TWO BRAVE WARRIORS WHO HAVE COME TO HELP ME...

DOGMATIX!

GRRROARRR!

VERY WELL, BUT GET ON WITH IT! THERE ISN'T MUCH TIME LEFT, AND CAESAR KEEPS NEEDLING ME. IF YOU SUCCEED THERE'LL BE GOLD ALL ROUND. IF NOT – THE CROCODILES!

AND I WARN YOU, EDIFIS, YOUR RIVAL ARTIFIS IS NOT PLEASED THAT I CHOSE YOU AND NOT HIM TO BUILD CAESAR'S PALACE. HE'D LOVE TO SEE YOU END UP INSIDE A CROCODILE. YOU MAY GO.

SHE LOOKS BAD TEMPERED, BUT SHE HAS A PRETTY NOSE...

VERY PRETTY!

COME HOME TO MY HOUSE...

IS THIS IT?

ER... YES. YES, I DESIGNED IT MYSELF.

THE DOOR'S JAMMED AGAIN... I MUST HAVE MADE A MISTAKE IN MY PLANS SOMEWHERE.

I'LL GIVE YOU A HAND.

CRASH!

OBELIX, NO!

NO, REALLY, IT'S QUITE ALL RIGHT! IT'S MORE USE THIS WAY!

POF! POF! POF!

ER... WATCH OUT FOR THE STEPS!

I GET THE IMPRESSION YOU REALLY DID NEED OUR HELP, EDIFIS.

THIS IS WHERE I WORK... MEET MY FAITHFUL SCRIBE EXLIBRIS. HE SPEAKS YOUR LANGUAGE FLUENTLY. HE SPEAKS ALL MODERN LANGUAGES – LATIN, GREEK, CELTIC, ETC...

IS IT A GOOD POSITION BEING A SCRIBE?

OH, IT'S VERY COMFORTABLE! I'M SITTING PRETTY – SQUATTING, RATHER!

HOW DOES ONE BECOME A SCRIBE?

I TOOK A CORRESPONDENCE COURSE... A VERY GOOD COLLEGE...

THE ADVERTISEMENT SAID, ANYONE WHO COULD DRAW COULD WRITE!

THE ARCHITECT ARTIFIS TO SEE ME? SHOW HIM IN!

EDIFIS, I'LL COME STRAIGHT TO THE POINT! LET US BUILD CAESAR'S PALACE TOGETHER. IF WE SUCCEED BEFORE THE DEADLINE WE'LL DIVIDE THE GOLD...

IF NOT, YOU CAN GO TO THE CROCODILES ON YOUR OWN! NO NEED TO GIVE THEM TWO WHERE ONE WILL DO!

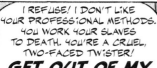

I REFUSE! I DON'T LIKE YOUR PROFESSIONAL METHODS. YOU WORK YOUR SLAVES TO DEATH. YOU'RE A CRUEL, TWO-FACED TWISTER!

GET OUT OF MY HOUSE!

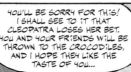

YOU'LL BE SORRY FOR THIS! I SHALL SEE TO IT THAT CLEOPATRA LOSES HER BET. YOU AND YOUR FRIENDS WILL BE THROWN TO THE CROCODILES, AND I HOPE THEY LIKE THE TASTE OF YOU...

?!?

BOING!

CLONK!

A BITING WIT, EH?

DOESN'T MINCE HIS WORDS!

POSITIVELY EATEN UP BY HATE!

HE REALLY SHOWED HIS TEETH!

DON'T USE THAT SORT OF LANGUAGE...

YOU KEEP REMINDING ME OF THE CROCODILES!

DOGMATIX!!!

COME AND VISIT THE BUILDING SITE INSTEAD. IT'S JUST OUTSIDE THE CITY GATES. I'LL SHOW YOU THE WAY WE BUILD THINGS HERE...

BRADABOOM!

?!

DURING THE LENTIL* BREAK THE LABOURERS HAVE AN UNEXPECTED VISITOR...

* A VERY POPULAR ANCIENT EGYPTIAN DISH

?! !?!
?! ?!?
? ?!
?

...WHOSE REMARKS ARE EVIDENTLY OF ABSORBING INTEREST.

TEEHEEHEE!

AND AT THE END OF THE LENTIL BREAK...

BOUHOU! OUHO!

...THE LABOURERS MAKE IT PERFECTLY CLEAR...

...THAT THEY ARE NOT GOING BACK TO WORK.

MASTER! THE LABOURERS WON'T GO ON WITH THE JOB! I THINK SOMEONE'S BEEN STIRRING THEM UP AGAINST YOU!

?

ALL THESE WORRIES ARE POSITIVELY BLOOD-CURDLING! BY THE TIME THE CROCODILES GET ME I'LL BE QUITE UNEATABLE!

ALL THE BETTER! ARE YOU SO KEEN TO MAKE THEM A GOOD MEAL?

BUT THOSE ARE SACRED CROCODILES! YOU CAN'T JUST FEED THEM ANY OLD THING!

THESE EGYPTIANS ARE CRAZY!

TAP! TAP! TAP!

IT WORKS LIKE MAGIC!

THAT'S RIGHT! TELL YOUR MEN TO QUEUE UP AND I'LL GIVE EVERYONE A DOSE OF MY MAGIC POTION.

NO.

OH, ALL RIGHT.

NO!

HOWEVER DID HE MANAGE TO PENETRATE MY DISGUISE?

AND NOW THE WORK GOES HAPPILY FORWARD, TO AN ACCOMPANIMENT OF SINGING, JOKES AND PUNS, UNFORTUNATELY UNTRANSLATABLE...

GETTING ON NICELY!

SLURP! SLURP!

GRRRRRRRRR

?

GRRRRRRRRRRR

* YELP! YELP! YELP!

13

THESE AMAZING FOREIGN WIZARDS WILL END UP HELPING EDIFIS TO WIN! I MUST DO SOMETHING!

KRUKHUT!

WHAT IS IT, ARTIFIS, MY MASTER?

I KNOW EDIFIS IS EXPECTING A CONSIGNMENT OF STONE TO COME DOWN THE NILE FROM THE COUNTRY. THAT STONE MUST NEVER REACH THE BUILDING SITE... HERE'S GOLD TO SETTLE THE BUSINESS!

KRUKHUT MEETS THE FLEET BRINGING STONE FOR THE PALACE, AND HIS GOLD QUICKLY OVERCOMES THE CAPTAIN'S SCRUPLES...

* UNLOAD THOSE STONES!

* NOT ON THE BANK! THE OTHER SIDE!

BONK!

THE LABOURERS, NATIVES OF THE RURAL DISTRICTS OF EGYPT, OBEY WITHOUT QUESTION.

SPLOSH!

SPLASH!

14

* BAIN'T NO USE ARGUFYING WITH HE!

* OI RECKON GAFFER BE CRAZY!

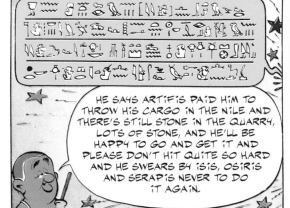

SOON AFTERWARDS

WE SHALL BE JOINING THE NILE AND THEN FOLLOWING THE RIVER SOUTH.

MEANWHILE, IN THE HOUSE OF THE INFAMOUS ARTIFIS...

I'VE LEARNT THAT THOSE MIRACLE-WORKING FOREIGNERS HAVE GONE OFF TO GET MORE STONE. KRUKHUT, THEY MUST NOT RETURN! THIS IS WHAT YOU HAVE TO DO...

THE FLEET GLIDES SLOWLY DOWN THE MAJESTIC AND SACRED RIVER NILE...

THIS IS SLOW!

VERY SLOW!

TOO SLOW!

ALL MOVE TO THE BANK! FASTEN THE BOATS FIRMLY TOGETHER WITH ROPES!

A BIT OF EXERCISE AT LAST!

BY TOUTATIS, THAT BOY NEVER CEASES TO SURPRISE ME, EVEN THOUGH I DO KNOW HE FELL INTO A CAULDRON FULL OF MAGIC POTION WHEN HE WAS A BABY!

AT NIGHTFALL THEY CAMP ON THE RIVER BANK...

LENTILS AGAIN! NOT A SINGLE SLICE OF BOAR! AND THEN THEY'LL WONDER WHY I'VE COME OVER WEAK!

TOMORROW WE'LL VISIT THE SPHINX AND THE PYRAMIDS. IT'S NOT FAR AWAY, AND THEY'RE WORTH SEEING!

BUT UNDER COVER OF DARKNESS A CUNNING SPY IS WATCHING AND WAITING.

TEE HEE HEE!

125

WELL DONE, OBELIX! OH, VERY WELL DONE!

POP! POP! POP!

SNIFF?

PERHAPS WE COULD STICK IT ON AGAIN?

YOU'RE ALWAYS BREAKING THINGS! IT'S LUCKY NO ONE SAW US. THE ONLY THING TO DO IS BURY THAT NOSE IN THE SAND.

SOON AFTERWARDS

THERE!

NO ONE WILL EVER THINK OF DIGGING HERE.

DOGMATIX!

COME ON, GETAFIX, WE MUSTN'T STOP HERE! I'LL EXPLAIN!

EXPLAIN? WHAT FOR?

BUT MY PORTRAIT'S NOT FINISHED!

?

PITY... IT WAS A GOOD LIKENESS, SPECIALLY THE SPHINX...

...THE SPHINX!

SOUVEN

TAP! TAP!

SO NOW YOU KNOW WHY THE SPHINX HAS NO NOSE. WHICH IS A PITY, FOR THE SPHINX'S NOSE, LOST TO THIS DAY, WAS A VERY FINE SPECIMEN OF A NOSE, IF NOT SO BEAUTIFUL AS CLEOPATRA'S, WHICH, AS WE BELIEVE WE MENTIONED BEFORE, WAS A VERY PRETTY NOSE INDEED.

TAP! TAP! TAP! TAP! TAP! TAP! TAP! TAP! TAP! TAP! TAP! TAP! TAP! TAP! TAP! TAP! TAP! TAP!

INSIDE THE PYRAMID...

MY POWERS ARE NOT STRONG ENOUGH TO GET US OUT OF HERE... I AM VERY MUCH AFRAID THIS MAY BE THE END OF OUR ADVENTURES, BY BELENOS!

I'M ONLY SORRY FOR EDIFIS... WITHOUT OUR HELP HE'LL END UP INSIDE A CROCODILE.

WELL, I'M SORRY FOR MY POOR LITTLE DOGMATIX... AREN'T I, DOGMATIX?

DOGMATIX?!

YES, DOGMATIX! WHAT ABOUT IT? YOU'RE NOT GOING TO BE CROSS WITH ME FOR BRINGING HIM? ANYWAY, I DIDN'T BRING HIM, HE CAME ALL BY HIMSELF!

EXACTLY! HE'S FOUND US THANKS TO HIS NOSE... IN WHICH CASE HE CAN FIND HIS WAY BACK AGAIN AND SHOW US THE WAY OUT!

BY BELENOS, YOU'RE RIGHT!

DOGMATIX, IF YOU HELP US OUT OF HERE YOU'LL GET A VERY BIG BONE OUTSIDE!

YOU'LL GET TWO BIG BONES!

HEAPS OF BIG BONES!

OBELIX, I APOLOGIZE! YOU WERE QUITE RIGHT TO BRING YOUR DOGGIE!

SOMETIMES I FEEL HE UNDERSTANDS EVERYTHING I SAY!

1 THE FOREIGNERS HAVE DISAPPEARED, THERE'S NO NEED FOR YOU TO GO ON WITH YOUR JOURNEY.
2 I GOT IT FIRST TIME.

IT'S MAGIC! YOU'RE WIZARDS! ONLY A SUPERMAN COULD EVER FIND HIS WAY OUT OF...

WHAM!

THE BOATS SET OFF AGAIN AND SAIL PEACEFULLY ON UP THE NILE...

SCRUNCH! SCRUNCH! SCRUNCH!

...STOPPING OFF TO SEE THE SIGHTS AT INTERESTING SPOTS SUCH AS LUXOR...

NO, NO, AND FOR THE THIRD TIME NO, OBELIX! THAT THING IN THE MIDDLE OF THE VILLAGE? IT WOULD JUST LOOK SILLY.

WE SHALL NEVER BE IN CONCORD OVER THIS!

MEANWHILE, BACK AT ALEXANDRIA...

O ARTIFIS, MY MASTER... THEY'RE WIZARDS! THEY HAVE SUPERHUMAN POWERS!

!?

THEY'VE MANAGED TO GET OUT OF THE LABYRINTH OF THE GREAT PYRAMID!

FANTASTIC! THEY'RE JUST FANTASTIC!

ALL THE MORE REASON TO FIND SOME WAY OF STOPPING THEM! EDIFIS MUST NOT BUILD THAT PALACE, KRUKHUT!

AFTER A VOYAGE OF MANY STADIA*

MY FRIENDS! BACK AT LAST!

AND WE'VE BROUGHT YOU ENOUGH STONE TO FINISH THE PALACE!

* STADIUM: ROMAN MEASURE OF ABOUT 184 METRES. AS THERE ARE 30·48 CENTIMETRES IN A FOOT, AND 12 FEET IN AN ALEXANDRINE, IT IS EASY TO WORK OUT THAT THERE ARE ABOUT 50½ ALEXANDRINES IN ONE STADIUM.

THE LABOURERS, WELL DOSED WITH MAGIC POTION, WORK SWIFTLY

IF I WASN'T HERE TO CORRECT THESE PLANS...

I'VE JUST HEARD THAT CLEOPATRA'S COMING TO VISIT THE BUILDING SITE!

SURE ENOUGH...

OH, DON'T STOP! I'M JUST PAYING A QUIET VISIT, INCOGNITO. DO GO ON!

THERE'S NO DENYING IT, SHE DOES HAVE A PRETTY NOSE!

A VERY PRETTY NOSE!

DID YOU SEE HER NOSE, DOGMATIX?

MEANWHILE, IN ARTIFIS'S HOUSE...

AN IDEA! I NEED AN IDEA!

HELP ME! **AND FOR THE LAST TIME GO AND SHAVE YOUR HEAD!**

I CAN'T, MASTER. I MADE A VOW...

I'VE GOT IT! IT'S A PIECE OF CAKE!

SLAP!

23

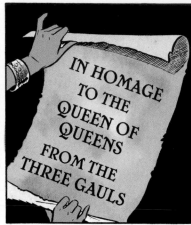

132

WHAT DO WE DO NOW? SHALL WE BASH THEM?

DON'T DO ANYTHING! IF YOU RESIST CLEOPATRA YOU'LL BE HEADING FOR DISASTER!

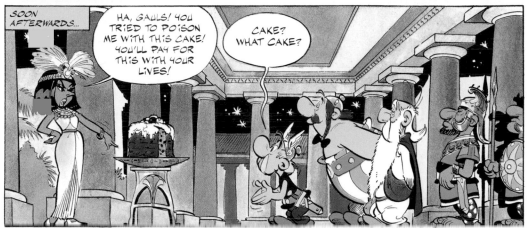

SOON AFTERWARDS...

HA, GAULS! YOU TRIED TO POISON ME WITH THIS CAKE! YOU'LL PAY FOR THIS WITH YOUR LIVES!

CAKE? WHAT CAKE?

BRING IN MY TASTER!

SNAP!

HE TASTED A BIT OF THAT CAKE, AND NOW LOOK AT HIM!

IT'S ALL A MISTAKE, BY TOUTATIS! WE'RE INNOCENT!

* OOH, OOH, OOH!

I DON'T WANT TO HEAR ANOTHER WORD!

BUT...

IF THE QUEEN DOESN'T WANT TO HEAR ANOTHER WORD IT'S NO GOOD SAYING ANOTHER WORD, ASTERIX... FOR NOW!

TAKE THEM AWAY! AND GIVE THE SACRED CROCODILES THEIR APERITIF!

BUT WHY WOULDN'T YOU LET US EXPLAIN?

I HAVE AN IDEA...

BESIDES, YOU CAN'T ARGUE WITH CLEOPATRA... SHE'S GOT A FOUL TEMPER, BUT SUCH A PRETTY NOSE!

DRINK THIS, TASTER. YOU'LL FEEL BETTER!

OH, SO THUMPING THEM IS ALL RIGHT BUT EATING ALMONDS ISN'T?

THERE'S A TIME FOR THUMPING PEOPLE AND A TIME FOR EATING ALMONDS! THAT'S GOOD MANNERS!

* GLUG, GLUG, GLUG

I FEEL BETTER... MUCH BETTER...

WHY, I FEEL FINE! I'M HUNGRY!

THAT CAKE HAD NOTHING TO DO WITH YOUR TASTER'S ILLNESS, O QUEEN. HE JUST HAS A DELICATE STOMACH FROM EATING TOO MUCH RICH FOOD!

I HAVE TREATED YOU UNJUSTLY, O GAULS! YOU SHALL GO FREE! AS FOR THIS TASTER, WHOSE STOMACH HAS CAUSED ME, THE QUEEN OF QUEENS, TO MAKE A MISTAKE, I DISMISS HIM!

THERE WAS ENOUGH POISON IN THAT CAKE FOR A WHOLE COHORT OF LEGIONARIES. IT'S A GOOD THING WE DRANK MY ANTIDOTE...

I SAY, THANK YOU VERY MUCH! I FOUND THE JOB OF TASTER VERY DISTASTEFUL... IT WAS POISONING MY LIFE.

WELL, I'M OFF! IT'S TIME I HAD SOMETHING TASTY!

LET'S GET BACK TO THE BUILDING SITE. WE MUST FIND OUT WHO WAS RESPONSIBLE FOR THIS OUTRAGE!

ASTERIX, WHAT IS AN ANTIDOTE?

AND AT THE BUILDING SITE...

DOGMATIX! YOU NEARLY KNOCKED ME OVER!

THANK RA YOU'RE BACK! MY MASTER EDIFIS DISAPPEARED IMMEDIATELY AFTER YOU WERE ARRESTED!

!!!

138

I'VE SEEN AMAZING THINGS GOING ON AT THAT SITE, O CAESAR! THE LABOURERS DRINK A MAGIC POTION WHICH GIVES THEM ENORMOUS STRENGTH AND LETS THEM PICK UP VERY HEAVY LOADS QUITE EASILY. I DRANK SOME OF IT!

IT OCCURS TO ME, MINTJULEP, THAT YOU MAY HAVE DRUNK SOMETHING ELSE TOO...

SO YOU DON'T BELIEVE ME, CAESAR? I'M A WEAK, PUNY, DELICATE TYPE, BUT I BET I CAN BEAT THE STRONGEST MAN IN YOUR BODYGUARD!

HERE, SUPERFLUOUS, COME AND PUT THIS FELLOW IN HIS PLACE

SNAP!

HA! HA! HA! HA! HA!

PAF! ★

HA! HA! HA! HA! HA! HA! HA!

?!

HMM... ALL RIGHT, SUPERFLUOUS, YOU MAY GO, THANK YOU!

HA! HA! HA! HA! HA! HA!

SO YOU WEREN'T LYING... YET I ONLY KNOW ONE MAN WHO CAN BREW SUCH A POTION...

AND HE'S A LONG WAY AWAY... A GAULISH DRUID...

A GAULISH DRUID ?!?

THERE ARE SOME GAULS ON THE BUILDING SITE. THREE OF THEM.

WHAT? AN OLD DRUID WITH A WHITE BEARD, A CUNNING LITTLE ONE AND A STUPID GREAT OAF!

THAT'S THEM, O CAESAR.

ASTERIX, OBELIX AND GETAFIX, THE INVINCIBLE GAULS. THEY CAN PERFORM ANY MIRACLE... I MUST DO SOMETHING!

141

* ANCIENT GAULISH WAR-SONG

142

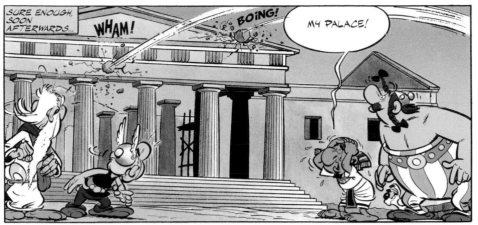

SURE ENOUGH, SOON AFTERWARDS...

WHAM!

BOING!

MY PALACE!

WE'LL HAVE TO LET CLEOPATRA KNOW! SHE MUST HAVE ENOUGH INFLUENCE OVER CAESAR TO GET THIS ATTACK STOPPED.

GOOD IDEA! EXLIBRIS! WRITE THE QUEEN A MESSAGE.

NOW THEN... NO SPELLING MISTAKES...
👁 BEFORE 🦉
EXCEPT AFTER 〰

TCHONK!

DOGMATIX WILL CARRY THE MESSAGE TO CLEOPATRA!

DOGMATIX?!

BUT DOGMATIX IS ONLY A PUPPY!

MAYBE, BUT HE'S VERY INTELLIGENT!

HERE'S THE MESSAGE!

YOU'LL SEE!

?

SEEK, DOGMATIX! CLEOPATRA! SEEK!

?

I TOLD YOU HE WAS TOO YOUNG TO UNDERSTAND!

TOO YOUNG! A LITTLE DOG WHO CAN BEG SO NICELY, AND SO ON...

THERE, THERE, OBELIX, DON'T BE CROSS! I WAS ONLY TEASING. I'LL SHOW HIM THE RIGHT WAY MYSELF!

FANCY SAYING MY DOG'S NO GOOD!

QUICK, GETAFIX, WHILE OBELIX ISN'T LOOKING! GIVE ME A GOOD SWIG OF MAGIC POTION!

RHUBARBRHUBARBRHU... BARBRHUB ARBRHUBARBRHU...

SOON AFTERWARDS

OFF WE GO, DOGMATIX!

?

WATCH OUT! ONE OF THE BESIEGED MEN IS TRYING TO BREAK IN AGAIN!

WHOOSH!

HERE YOU ARE, OBELIX! DOGMATIX HAS JUST GOT BACK! HE DID HIS JOB PERFECTLY!

THERE YOU ARE! YOU SEE?

LET'S HOPE THE QUEEN ACTS QUICKLY. THE ROMAN MISSILES ARE DESTROYING THE PALACE!

SURE ENOUGH, IN THE CAMP OF THE BESIEGING ARMY...

THERE YOU ARE, CAESAR! EVEN IF WE DON'T CAPTURE THEM THE PALACE WILL BE DESTROYED JUST THE SAME!

EXCELLENT, OPERACHORUS, EXCELLENT!

AVE, CAESAR... ER... SOMEONE WANTS TO SPEAK TO YOU...

WHO IS IT?

ZING! BOOM!

TAPTAPTAP! TAPTAPTAP!

TANTANTARA!!!

?!?

ER... QUEEN... MY DEAR QUEEN...

THAT'S ENOUGH OF THAT! WHEN I HEARD WHAT WAS HAPPENING I HURRIED OUT OF THE PALACE AT ONCE! I DIDN'T EVEN STOP TO CHANGE!

OOPS!

WHEN YOU MAKE A BET YOU MUST PLAY FAIR AND I HAD A RIGHT TO CALL IN THE GAULS AND I'LL PROVE TO YOU THAT EGYPTIANS CAN BUILD BEAUTIFUL PALACES...

...AND I ABSOLUTELY INSIST THAT THE ROMANS LEAVE THE BUILDERS IN PEACE AND REPAIR ALL THE DAMAGE THEY'VE DONE BEFORE LEAVING AND IT'S A CRYING SHAME...

...AND...

ALL RIGHT! ALL RIGHT! DON'T GO ON! I'M SORRY AND I'LL DO WHAT YOU WANT...

ZING! BOOM! TANTANTARA!

PHEW!

WELL... ER... NOW WHAT DO WE DO?

RAISE THE SIEGE AND REPAIR THE DAMAGE YOU'VE DONE, IDIOT!

AVE!

AFTER ALL, I WOULDN'T WANT CLEOPATRA TO TURN HER NOSE UP AT ME!

A VERY PRETTY NOSE, IN CASE WE DIDN'T MENTION IT BEFORE...

LOOK! THE ROMANS ARE RAISING THE SIEGE, BY BELENOS!

VICTORY, BY TOUTATIS!

AND ALL THANKS TO WHO?

148

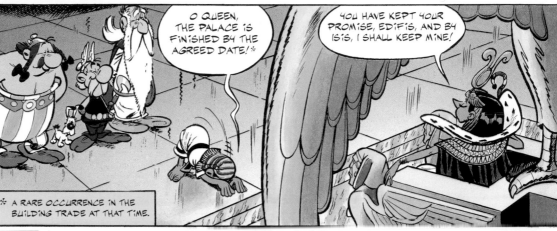

* A RARE OCCURRENCE IN THE BUILDING TRADE AT THAT TIME.

NEXT DAY...

NOT A BAD PALACE, IS IT?

HERE THEY ARE!

WHERE?

FOR YOU TO CUT THE RIBBON, O CAESAR!

O LOVELIEST OF QUEENS, YOURS IS THE HONOUR OF CUTTING THE RIBBON WHICH PROVES THAT I HAVE LOST MY BET, BY JUPITER! I YIELD WITH A GOOD GRACE BEFORE SO MUCH GRACE.

THE CROWD ACCLAIM THEIR QUEEN, INVOKING THE SUN-GOD OF EGYPT...

RA! RA! RA! RA! R

NOW WHO KNOWS BEST?

THAT'S A PRETTY KNOWS!

AT A BANQUET FOR 14,000 GUESTS (IT HAD BEEN PLANNED TO INVITE 13,000, BUT EGYPTIANS ARE SUPERSTITIOUS)...

YOU'VE SAVED MY LIFE AND TAUGHT ME MY JOB... MY GOLD IS YOURS!

NO, NO, IT WAS A PLEASURE. WHAT ARE YOU PLANNING NOW?

I'M FRIENDS WITH ARTIFIS AGAIN...

...TOGETHER WE'LL BUILD THE FINEST PYRAMIDS WITH THE SHARPEST POINTS IN EGYPT!

LATER, IN CLEOPATRA'S PALACE...

OUR WORK IS FINISHED. WE HAVE COME TO SAY GOODBYE, O QUEEN.

THAT NOSE...

YOU HAVE PERFORMED MIRACLES, GAULS, AND YOU ARE ENTITLED TO ALL THE GRATITUDE OF THE QUEEN OF QUEENS: ME!

I AM MAKING YOU A PRESENT OF THESE PRECIOUS MANUSCRIPTS FROM THE LIBRARY OF ALEXANDRIA O DRUID...

YOUR NOSE... ER... YOUR MAJESTY IS TOO CHARMING, BY BELENOS...

WHAT A NOSE!

IT SEEMS VERY LITTLE FOR ALL THE HELP YOU HAVE GIVEN ME. I DON'T KNOW HOW TO THANK YOU...

ALWAYS AT YOUR SERVICE... AND IF YOU EVER NEED ANYTHING ELSE BUILT IN EGYPT — SAY A CANAL BETWEEN THE RED SEA AND THE MEDITERRANEAN...

...WELL, CALL ON SOMEONE FROM OUR COUNTRY, BY TOUTATIS!

SOON AFTERWARDS...

NICE OF CLEOPATRA TO LEND US HER OWN BARGE TO TAKE US BACK TO GAUL...

AND THE CAPTAIN GIVES THE ORDER TO GO...

*FULL SPEED AHEAD!

DING! DING!

BOOM

DO YOU THINK WE'LL MEET THOSE PIRATES AGAIN, ASTERIX?

I DON'T KNOW, OBELIX, BUT I GET THE FEELING THEY'RE NOT FAR AWAY!

SURE ENOUGH, DOWN IN THE HOLD...

I HAD TO TAKE THIS JOB TO PAY FOR MY LAST BOAT, BUT AS SOON AS I CAN PUT A DEPOSIT DOWN ON ANOTHER I'LL LOOK FOR THOSE CONFOUNDED GAULS!

AFTER A LUXURY CRUISE LASTING SEVERAL WEEKS...

SCRENCH!

SCRUNCH!

...THEY AT LAST SIGHT...

A SAIL! A SAIL! ASTERIX, OBELIX AND GETAFIX ARE BACK!

I WILL NOW COMPOSE A LITTLE SONG...

THE GAULISH VILLAGE WELCOMES HOME ITS HEROES WITH ITS USUAL ENTHUSIASM AND FEASTING...

...AND IT WAS ALL THANKS TO DOGMATIX!

A NOSE, MY DEAR FELLOW, WHAT A NOSE!

AND FOR THE NEXT FEW DAYS, EVERYONE IS HAPPY.... AT LEAST, NEARLY EVERYONE...

NO, OBELIX. NO!

I DON'T LIKE THE DESIGN OF YOUR NEW MENHIRS! LET'S KEEP IT GAULISH!

THE END

UDERZO

152